Cursed with a poor sense of direction and a propensity to read, **Annie Claydon** spent much of her childhood lost in books. A degree in English Literature followed by a career in computing didn't lead directly to her perfect job—writing romance for Mills & Boon—but she has no regrets in taking the scenic route. She lives in London: a city where getting lost can be a joy.

Also by Annie Claydon

Healed by the Single Dad Doc
From Doctor to Princess?
Firefighter's Christmas Baby
Resisting Her English Doc
Festive Fling with the Single Dad
Best Friend to Royal Bride
Winning the Surgeon's Heart

London Heroes miniseries

Falling for Her Italian Billionaire
Second Chance with the Single Mum

Discover more at millsandboon.co.uk.

A RIVAL TO STEAL HER HEART

ANNIE CLAYDON

MILLS & BOON

First published in Great Britain 2020
by Mills & Boon, an imprint of Harper*Collins**Publishers*
1 London Bridge Street, London, SE1 9GF

Large Print edition 2020

ISBN: 978-0-263-08599-0

This book is produced from independently certified FSC™ paper to ensure responsible forest management. For more information visit www.harpercollins.co.uk/green.

Printed and bound in Great Britain
by CPI Group (UK) Ltd, Croydon, CR0 4YY

CHAPTER ONE

THE YOUNG MAN had a mop of red-brown hair, blue eyes and an easy, engaging smile. Anna Caulder thought she'd seen everything, but the tattoos on the backs of his hands plumbed the depths of bad taste.

'This may hurt a little, Callum. Tell me if it gets too much, and we'll stop.'

'That's all right, *Miss* Caulder.' Callum gave her a cheery smile. Someone must have told him that, as a surgeon, Anna should be addressed as 'Miss' and he was clearly eager to please. 'This place is pretty cool.'

Unfortunately that wasn't going to make removing the tattoos any less painful. Anna's expertise might, but only if Callum could be persuaded to stop looking around at the gleaming worktops and state-of-the-art medical equipment, and keep still.

'I'm going to need you to take a couple of deep breaths, and relax, Callum.'

'Okay. Are you going to do both hands?'

'Just one will be enough for this session, Cal. You'll need some time to heal afterwards,' Dr Jamie Campbell-Clarke interrupted. He did that a lot.

'Are you supposed to be here?' By Anna's calculations, today was a Monday, which was one of the three days a week that Jamie Campbell-Clarke spent working in the A&E department of a nearby hospital. Thursdays and Fridays were usually the days when she could expect to see him here, at the London Central Clinic, accompanying one of the teenagers he'd referred from the youth charity he ran in Hastings.

'I'm only at the hospital for two days this week. So I thought I'd come along and watch you work.' He sounded positively gleeful at the prospect.

'And make sure I didn't bottle out,' Callum reminded him.

'Yeah. There was that to it, as well.'

Jamie's charity aimed to help teenagers like Callum overcome all kinds of disadvantages and make the most of their lives. He was fiercely protective of his young charges, and checked on everything. Which was fine, because he was an excellent doctor, but a trace of professional rivalry sometimes crept into his exchanges with Anna.

'It would get it over with quicker. To do both hands.' Callum's face took on an imploring look.

'Miss Caulder will do as much as she can…' Anna turned and shot Jamie a glare and he fell silent, hopefully remembering that this was *her* consulting room and plastic surgery was *her* speciality.

'I know you want to get rid of these tattoos, Callum…' Anna glanced at the spidery words and the suggestive poses of the stick figures, and looked away quickly '…but it needs to be done properly, which is going to take a little more time than it did to get them.'

Callum nodded, staring at the backs of his hands. 'Yeah, I know. Jamie explained it all… At least they're black ink, so that's easier to get rid of, isn't it?'

'Yes, that's right. But I'm sure that Dr Campbell-Clarke explained that new tattoos are a little more difficult, and I gather you've only had these for a few months—'

'Twelve weeks,' Jamie interjected, and Anna ignored him. Heaven forfend he allowed her to get away with anything as vague as a *few months*.

Callum gave her a sudden smile. 'I understand. Thanks, Miss Caulder.'

He might not be thanking her at the end of the session, when his hand was hurting, but Callum didn't make a sound as she carefully traced the outline of the tattoos on the back of his right hand with the laser. When she'd finished, he gave her another smile, which smacked a little of false bravado.

'That's going to give us the best results we can achieve for today.' Anna decided that Callum needed a little reassurance that the short procedure was actually going to show some benefit. 'I think when the inflammation goes down, you'll see a big difference. Would you like the nurse to put a dressing on your other hand as well, just to cover the tattoos there?'

'Yeah. Thanks. It beats having to keep wearing gloves.'

'All right then. We'll give you some replacement dressings and a leaflet on how to care for your hand. That's really important, to avoid any infection.'

Callum nodded. 'Thanks, Miss Caulder. Jamie's already told me about that.'

'I'm sure he has. I'll leave it to him to check on your hand and re-dress it as necessary.' Out of the corner of her eye, she saw Jamie lay his hand on his chest, as if surprised that she'd finally found something that she could trust him to do.

Anna ignored the gesture. It was just a game that she and Dr Campbell-Clarke played. Each trying to outdo the other. Watching each other like hawks to make sure that the patients that he brought to her consulting room had the best possible treatment. It was harmless enough, and it took her mind off his eyes…

Moss green. On a woman, they'd be stunningly beautiful, and Jamie's dark hair and the strong line of his jaw made them seem like dazzling jewels, surrounded by steel and muscle. Under the clear lights of the consulting room they seemed almost luminescent.

But she had a policy of not thinking about his eyes. They were enough to make any woman's hand shake. Knowing that he was watching her every move and that he'd be quick to correct any mistakes gave her hand the professional, rock-steady quality that any surgeon needed.

He was wearing green today, a dark green flannel shirt with the sleeves rolled up. That was his style when carrying out the business of his charity, casual clothes and first names. It was a little different from the Dr Campbell-Clarke persona that Anna saw when she visited the large, central London hospital where he worked three days a week, but he had the same self-assurance. Thc same way of daring anyone to question him, which was perhaps why Anna never hesitated to do just that.

The nurse had dressed Callum's hands, and he was ready to stand now, a little shaky still from the procedure. Jamie ushered him outside, to where a neat-looking, middle-aged woman was sitting in the waiting room. Callum sat down beside her, and she gave him a brisk nod, but her hand moved to his back in a gesture of comfort.

'Mary, this is Miss Caulder.' Jamie introduced the two women quickly. 'Callum did really well, and Miss Caulder's very pleased with the results of the procedure.'

Anna could have said that herself. She resisted the urge to push him to one side, and smiled at the other woman. 'I've just done the one hand, and I think that when the inflammation goes down you'll see an appreciable difference. Callum asked us to dress his left hand as well, to cover it up.'

Mary nodded. 'Thank you, Miss Caulder.'

'I'll see him again in six weeks. I'm hoping we won't need too many sessions, and we should be able to remove the tattoos completely.'

'It's very good of you.' Mary frowned. 'I'm sorry—'

Jamie cut her short. 'It's okay. What's done is done and we look forward, eh, Callum?'

Callum nodded, his fingers moving to back of his right hand. Mary grabbed his hand, snatching it away before he could worry at the dressings.

'Maybe you'd like to sit for a while before you go.' The armchairs in the comfortable waiting room were laid out so that patients could sit in groups with their families, and

Anna gestured towards the side table. 'Help yourself to coffee or tea.'

'Thank you. I think we'd like a drink before we get back on the train…' Mary glanced at Callum and he nodded.

'Great. Well I'll see you in six weeks then, Callum.' Anna smiled at him, and Mary nudged him.

'Yes. Thanks, Miss Caulder.'

Jamie went to fetch Mary and Callum's drinks, and Anna turned away, walking back to the consulting room. All the teenagers that Jamie brought here had some kind of story, and Jamie's obvious concern for Callum showed that his probably wasn't a good one.

She heard a knock on the open door and turned.

'Nice job,' Jamie said from the doorway.

'Did you expect anything else?'

He shrugged and Anna took a gulp of air into her lungs. The to and fro between them didn't seem to be working as well as it usually did. Maybe because of the green shirt, which made the colour of his eyes so much more prominent.

'Ask. I know you want to.'

If he was going to add mind-reading to his talents, then Anna needed to establish a few more boundaries. But she *was* curious. She gestured towards the door, and Jamie walked into the room, closing it behind him.

'All right then. Callum seems a nice lad, and Mary doesn't look like the type to take any nonsense. What on earth is he doing with those tattoos?'

Jamie quirked his lips downwards. 'He *is* a very nice lad. Mary's his aunt, and she took him in two years ago. Before that, he was neglected and abused by his mother.'

'Poor kid. So he's acting up?'

'Yeah. His older brother turned up three months ago, and Callum disappeared with him. Mary was frantic, and tried everything she could think of to find him, that's how she made contact with us. He came back a week later, his brother had moved on and dumped him.'

'And that's where he got the tattoos?'

Jamie nodded. 'Callum craves acceptance, and like a lot of kids with his kind of background he has a few issues with impulse control. He just wants to please, and he doesn't think about the consequences. Our youth counsellor is working with him pretty intensively, and it's pretty clear that we don't know the full scope of what's happened to him yet.'

'You're getting to the bottom of it, though.'

'Yeah. We will. In the meantime, I just wanted to let you know that we're doing all we can to make sure that he won't be back with another set of tattoos that he regrets. And to…um…apologise. For any embarrassment.'

'I've seen worse. I didn't run out of the room screaming then either.'

'No. Of course. But your non-judgemental approach is just the kind of thing that Callum needs.'

Was that a *thank you*? Anna decided not to push it and ask. 'I'm just glad that they're a single colour and relatively superficial, so they shouldn't be too difficult to remove completely. Something like that won't help Callum when it comes to getting a job or a place in college. Or a girlfriend…'

'Yeah. He didn't grasp the full implications of some of them. Mary asked me to explain it to him…' His brow furrowed. Clearly he'd not found the conversation particularly easy.

'Well… Good luck with him…' The words slipped out before she'd had a chance to think. Jamie quirked his lips down.

'We don't leave things to luck.'

'No, I know. Hard work, determination and expertise.' Along with a lot of caring. Jamie's charity had a policy of tough love, and it worked. 'I'm actually not too proud to take a bit of luck when it comes my way.'

'I'll bear that in mind. Thanks for what you did today. I'll let you get on now.' He turned suddenly, closing the door behind him as he left.

Anna flopped down into her chair. Maybe Jamie was right, and luck didn't come into it. But there were some things that determination and hard work alone couldn't put right.

Maybe it was those eyes that were making her think this way. They tempted her to revisit a past that was done with, and couldn't be changed. If things had been different, then she might have allowed herself to get a little closer to Jamie. But they weren't different, and he probably wasn't interested in her anyway.

Think that. Keep thinking it.

She had no business lingering over Jamie

Campbell-Clarke's eyes, or his dedication, or the spark that fuelled their professional rivalry. Anna wasn't in the market for a relationship with him, or anyone else.

She'd fallen into that trap once before. As soon as things had started to get serious with Daniel, she'd told him that she couldn't have children, fully expecting him to leave. When he hadn't, she'd thought she had found that special someone who could accept her as she was. But after a year of marriage he'd changed his mind and left. Once was more than enough when it came to having her heart broken.

Anna puffed out a breath. Jamie was right in one thing. She had patients waiting and she had to get on.

Jamie's characteristically brusque two-line email had imparted the information that he'd visited Callum at home the previous evening, that he was in good spirits and that his Aunt Mary had reinforced the message that his gratitude for the help he was being given should take the form of not worrying at the dressings on his hand. He'd be back in six weeks and was looking forward to losing the unfortunate tattoos. Anna emailed a similarly brusque acknowledgement of the update, telling him to contact her if there was anything else she could do. She imagined there wouldn't be.

And this morning there were new challenges, the first of which didn't take a medical form. The private London Central Clinic was used to receiving patients whose fame required a degree of discretion and anonymity, but *this* patient had stretched policy almost to breaking point. She'd even caught her boss humming snatches of 'Everywhere'.

And the singer responsible for that rock classic was here. Even Anna felt a small flutter over meeting the man who had reached a million hearts, including her own, with the song.

'How's he doing?' She murmured the words to the ward receptionist, who leaned across her desk to whisper a reply.

'Just great. A little taller than I thought he'd be.'

Right. That wasn't the information Anna was after. 'He's settling in?'

'Oh, yes. They took him a cup of green tea and a biscuit.'

Asking what kind of biscuit would only stoke the fires. 'He has someone with him?'

'No, he came on his own. Just a driver and he didn't stay long. Parked on a meter, I expect.'

So fame didn't always guarantee companionship. It seemed a shame, though. 'Everywhere' had been the song that had spoken to Anna when her life had hit a rough patch, and she imagined she wasn't alone in that. It was all about hope, about kindling a flame in the darkness, to lead the way into the light.

'Okay, I'll go and see him now. Which room…?'

Jonny Campbell was sitting alone in his room. Dark glasses covered his eyes, and his head was nodding slightly to whatever was playing through his high-end headphones. His bag lay on the bed, unopened. One of the ward orderlies would unpack it for him if necessary, but Anna reckoned that Dr Lewis had told them to wait a short while, to see if he'd do it himself. Their patient was nominally here for assessment of burn scars on his arm and the side of his face, but Jon's listless indifference during his assessment interview had raised the possibility of mental health problems as well.

Dr Lewis had taken overall charge of his case, and Anna had been told to start treating the burns, but to be aware that there may be other issues.

'Hello. I'm Anna Caulder.'

Her words made him jump. Maybe his eyes had been closed under the glasses. Anna saw his hand shake as he removed his headphones.

'Hi. Jon Campbell.'

'I'm sorry if I startled you. You prefer Jon, or Jonny Campbell?'

His lips curved in a slow smile. 'Jonny Campbell's my professional name. Just Jon will do. You prefer Anna or Miss Caulder?'

'Anna will do.' He seemed so different from his stage persona. And yet somehow so familiar. Anna shook off the feeling. Her job was to find out what the real Jon Campbell needed, not the rock star Jonny Campbell.

'I think Dr Lewis prefers *Dr Lewis.* Or maybe sir…'

Anna laughed. The dry humour that Jonny Campbell put to such good use on stage was there still.

'Yes. I think he does. He's a great doctor, though.'

'I've no doubt of that. But he doesn't have your beautiful blue eyes.' Jon tilted his head towards her, and Anna blushed, fighting back the urge to tell him that she'd been to one of his concerts and loved his songs.

'Well I'm here to take care of your burns.' And to ignore compliments.

Jon flexed his arm. 'Yeah, that would be great. I didn't have much time to get them looked at when they happened, I was touring. I took a handful of painkillers and was back on stage the following evening. Being on stage in front of tens of thousands of people tends to make you forget about everything else.'

'And you never had a doctor look at them?'

'I was in hospital for a week in America. They said that my arm had become infected and gave me a course of antibiotics.'

'You went to hospital for the burns? I didn't see anything about that in your notes.'

'No, I…' Jon shrugged. 'I needed a break.'

If he'd been in hospital for a week, it sounded as if there was a bit more to it than that. 'Would it be okay if we contacted the hospital and asked them to send us through their notes?'

'Sure. Knock yourself out.'

'Thanks. I'll have our administrator follow that up with you.' Anna pulled up a seat, sitting down opposite Jon. 'Can you tell me what happened when you burned yourself?'

'One of the amps wasn't working. I kicked it, and it burst into flames.' Jon shook his head slowly. 'Serves me right. I guess there's a song there somewhere.'

'I'd like to hear it.' Anna bit her tongue. She'd resolved not to mention the songs.

'I'll sing it for you, Anna.'

Right. Another trace of Jonny Campbell's charm. But it was faded and worn, like a mask Jon assumed when he didn't want to face a reality that found him alone in a hospital room.

'Will someone be coming? To visit you...?' Maybe she was overstepping her boundaries a little, but the doctors here were given the time to get to know their patients as people, and were encouraged to do so.

'Didn't you know that I'm here incognito?'

'I did. That doesn't extend to family and friends, though, does it?'

'When you tour, all you have is the band. We've been having our differences lately. That's privileged information, by the way...'

'It's all privileged information here.'

'That's what everyone says.' Jon twisted his mouth. 'Then you see it in the papers the next morning.'

'It's not the way *we* do things.' Anna searched for eye contact and found none. She wished he'd take the glasses off, but guessed he wouldn't for a while at least. 'It's important that you understand that everything you say to us is completely confidential.'

Jon shrugged, as if it didn't really matter one way or the other.

'Blue-eyed Anna… It'd make a great song. Does that turn you on?' He was retreating again behind the rock star persona, expecting her to go weak at the knees. There was nothing like meeting your heroes to inject a dose of reality.

'Not particularly. Doing my job turns me on, and right now my interest in you is that you have scars that can be improved.'

Jon laughed suddenly, holding up his hands in a gesture of surrender. 'Okay, fair enough. My twin brother is just the same. Being a doctor turns *him* on.'

'You didn't ask for his help? With the burns?'

The back of her neck was prickling, and Anna ignored it. Two and two didn't always make four, and the feeling that she knew Jon Campbell was just an illusion, born from his fame.

'Nah. We don't talk. Jamie and I had a falling out.' Jon shrugged. 'He doesn't know I'm here, and he probably doesn't care. The rest of the family isn't much impressed with me either…'

'It's up to you but…sometimes families can surprise you.'

Jon shook his head, taking his glasses off, and suddenly there was no question about it. Anna's words dried in her throat. The jade-green eyes and ravaged face of Jonny Campbell really *were* familiar. His brother was Dr Jamie Campbell-Clarke.

CHAPTER TWO

MAYBE JON CAMPBELL had taken her wordless shock for granted, as the kind of thing that any woman would do when faced with a rock idol. Whatever. Anna couldn't think about that right now. She couldn't think about Jamie Campbell-Clarke either. What she *could* think about was her duties as a surgeon.

She asked Jon if she could examine his burns, and he nodded his assent, rolling up his sleeve. The skin was discoloured, beginning to tighten and contort, showing that the injuries had been given very little care.

It was odd. Whatever it was that made her heart beat a little faster when Jamie was in the room was entirely absent. Now that she'd made the connection, she could see that the brothers were very alike. Brown hair was brown hair and Jon's was longer than Jamie's, but they both had the same strong jaw, the same shaped face. And the eyes left no doubt, even if Jon's seemed just an unusual colour, while Jamie's were compelling.

She retreated to her seat, clasping her hands together. She had to remember that Jon was her patient, and act according to his wishes and in his best interests, even though her first thought was that Jamie would be horrified to find that his own brother was in the clinic and he didn't know it.

'I think that the scars can definitely be revised and improved, particularly the ones on your brow and neck. The one on your arm is a little bigger, but there's a lot we can do there as well.'

Jon nodded. 'Good. Thank you.'

Anna took a breath, wondering how best to ask. 'You said that Jonny Campbell is your professional name. Is your real name Campbell-Clarke, by any chance?'

'Yes, it is.' Jon shot her a questioning look. 'Not many people know me as Jon Campbell-Clarke any more…'

'So Dr Jamie Campbell-Clarke is your brother?'

A flash of defensiveness. 'Yeah. Looks a bit like me. We're not identical twins.'

'You both have the same colour eyes.'

'That'll be him then. You know him?'

'I do, and I should tell you that he sometimes visits this clinic.'

Jon nodded, pursing his lips. 'I didn't know that. Is that going to be a problem?'

'No. It's entirely up to you whether you want him to know you're here or not.' She should make that clear before she started to make the case for telling Jamie. 'I just thought that you should know.'

'Yeah. Thanks.' Jon heaved a sigh. 'When I said that we had a falling out… It was a pretty big one. And it was my fault, he has good reason to be angry with me.'

'Do you think he might also have good reason to forgive you?'

'Not particularly. Look…we were close once and now we're not. None of us gets to change the past.'

'Jamie might take issue with you there. He tries to change things for the kids he works with.'

'That's different.' She saw a flash of anger in Jon's face. 'Look. Sorry, but I can't…'

'It's okay. Just know that I'm here to help, and that I'll do whatever you want me to do.'

'Right. Well, you can tell him if you want. Or don't tell him, it's up to you. But I know what he'll say, and I don't want to hear it. Are we agreed?'

'Agreed. Is there anything else I can do for you?'

Jon heaved a sigh. 'I don't suppose there are any books in this place, are there? Not magazines, something I can get my teeth into.'

'Yes, we have a small collection. I'll send our activities co-ordinator in with a selection and if none of them appeal she'd be happy to go out and get you something that does.'

'Activities co-ordinator.' Jon gave a mock frown. 'She's not going to ask me to make raffia baskets, is she?'

Anna chuckled. 'Raffia baskets don't turn you on?'

'Not even a little bit. I'd like some fresh air...'

'We have a small garden area on the roof. It's secluded and the air's about as fresh as it gets anywhere in central London.'

'Sounds good to me. Jamie's not going to find me up there, is he?'

'No. He's not expected here for the rest of the week, and after that…we'll handle things.'

'Still thinking you might engineer a reconciliation?' Jon raised one eyebrow. 'I can save you a bit of time there, because you won't. Just handle it so that neither of us gets any nasty surprises.'

'All right. Consider it done.'

Lunchtime. Anna pulled on her coat, grabbed an energy bar from her desk drawer, and hurried out of the building. She'd already thought of about a thousand reasons why she shouldn't do this…

Families were out of her sphere of expertise, she knew that. She was the only child of two only children, and the large, extended family she'd married into had sometimes baffled her but mostly delighted her. She'd lost them when she and Daniel had divorced…

The clinic was her family now. Anna always did her best for the families of the patients who passed through, and now Jamie Campbell-Clarke came under that umbrella. It meant crossing the line that she'd drawn between professional and personal with him, but she couldn't step aside and do nothing.

He was sitting alone in the office he shared with two other doctors, the door wide open, and when he saw her he smiled. 'You wanted to see me?'

Why did that always sound like a challenge? Anna swallowed whatever smart retort was about to reach the tip of her tongue. Not the time for it.

'Yes, I did.' Anna sat down on the other side of his desk, keeping her coat on and clutching her handbag in her lap. 'Can we have a private conversation?'

Something kindled in his eyes and Anna ignored it. Jamie closed the door, sitting back down again. 'Sure…'

'We have a new patient at the clinic. He has some recent burn scars for revision, and…he has a demanding job, which has caused a great deal of emotional strain recently.

Jamie nodded. 'And who is this mystery patient? One of your celebrities?'

'Yes.'

He gave her a searching look. 'So you're not going to give me a name.'

Not until she'd reassured Jamie that Jon's condition was stable and he wasn't in any danger. 'He booked himself in earlier this morning. He's being well looked after, and there's no need for any concern.'

'That's always nice to know.' Jamie shot her a puzzled look, leaning back in his seat. He'd obviously decided that she'd get to the point sooner or later, and that he'd wait.

'It's your brother. Jon.'

Jamie's face hardened suddenly. Whatever it was between the two brothers, it was serious. She'd never seen Jamie look so thunderously angry.

'He asked you to come and see me?'

'No. I… He said he had a twin brother, but that there was some bad blood between you. When I realised it was you he was talking about, I told him I knew you and said that I thought you should know he was at the clinic. He seems…alone.'

Anna lapsed into silence. Maybe she'd got this all wrong. Maybe she should have listened to Jon when he'd told her that there was only one answer that Jamie would give to any plea for reconciliation. But Jamie never turned anyone away. It was a matter of pride that his charity would at least try to help any kid that knocked on its door.

'Okay. Thank you.'

That was it? 'I'm sorry if this… I didn't mean to overstep any boundaries.'

Suddenly the boundaries that she and Jamie had drawn had changed and Anna felt crushed within them. She should probably go now, and hope that Jamie would forget this had ever happened.

'That's okay. Jon knows you're here?'

'He said that I could tell you he was at the clinic, but I wasn't to tell him your reaction. He thinks you'll refuse to see him.' Right now that seemed to have been a forward-looking strategy on Jon's part.

'Right. It's good of you to let me know. Is that all?'

That was a clear invitation for her to leave. Anna wanted to ask what Jamie was going to do, even hint that he might tell her how he was feeling about this. But the hard mask of his face left her in no doubt that he'd just tell her to mind her own business.

'Yes. I'd better be going. I have to be back at the clinic in forty-five minutes.'

It was surprisingly hard to get up and leave. She'd come here intending to deliver a message, but now she badly wanted Jamie to let her in and allow her to help him. But he already seemed to have forgotten that she was in the room. As Anna closed the door behind her, he was staring at his hands, which were clenched into fists in front of him on the desk.

Jon. It had to happen sooner or later, and in truth Jamie was surprised that he hadn't bumped into his twin brother before now. But Jon's career only took him on flying visits to London, and hardly ever to Hastings. And in the three years since they'd argued, their family had tactfully contrived to keep them apart.

And the first person who'd brought him news of Jon, beyond what he tried to stop himself from reading in the paper, was Anna. Jamie's first thought had been to lock her in his office until she promised never to set eyes on Jon again. To protect her…

He reminded himself that Anna could look after herself. She'd proved that to him time and time again, meeting him headlong and refusing to back down when she knew she was right about something. She wasn't going to fall for the good looks and the rock star charm.

Jamie shook his head, trying not to think about it. Women *did* fall for Jon. Jamie's own fiancée had fallen for him, and Jon had done what probably came perfectly naturally to him as a rock star, and what any brother would have found unthinkable. Jon could have had any woman he wanted, but he'd taken the one that Jamie had wanted.

Three years. He could still feel the anger and the shock. The clawing pain that two people who he'd loved could have betrayed him like that.

Did that outweigh the thirty-odd years that had gone before? Growing up together, doing everything together? Looking out for each other? His parents and sister had made it very clear that they wouldn't force a reconciliation and that if Jamie didn't want to take the first step they didn't blame him. They probably didn't know that Jon was in the clinic either.

It was probably better to let sleeping dogs lie. But the childhood refrain, whenever Jon had been hurt or upset, wouldn't stop echoing through his thoughts.

What did you do now, little brother?

It was relatively normal to go for weeks without seeing Jamie Campbell-Clarke. But as luck would have it—and Anna wasn't sure whether the luck was good or bad—he was waiting for her the following morning when she walked into the A&E department of the hospital.

She'd been worrying all night about whether she'd done the right thing. But Jamie hadn't come to the clinic to see his brother so she should do as she'd been asked and let it go. That was easier said than done.

'Hi. Thanks for coming.' He looked very tired.

She'd seen Jamie tired before—his schedule was impressively busy—but today his face reminded her of Jon's haggard features. It didn't look as though he'd had much sleep either.

'My pleasure.' They had work to do, and she should concentrate on that.

'I didn't know you had an interest in syndactyly.' He too seemed anxious to keep this professional.

'I studied under Sir Max Barnes in Manchester for a while.'

'Ah. That explains it.'

It really didn't need any explanation. The clinic made the services of its doctors available to nearby hospitals on a regular basis, as part of an ongoing partnership programme. Jamie would have consulted the list and found Anna's name on it. That was all there was to it. Jon had had nothing to do with his call to the clinic to ask if she might give a second opinion on one of his patients. All the same, there was a formal unease about Jamie's manner that wasn't like him.

The best thing to do was to ignore it. She followed him to a cubicle where a nurse was sitting with a baby.

'This little fella was brought in early this morning. He was abandoned and the police are looking for the mother.' Jamie's face was impassive, but his eyes reflected the same compassion that showed in the nurse's face. In an environment where every case had a story behind it, some were still easier to deal with than others.

'I've examined him, and he's generally surprisingly healthy. But I wanted a second opinion on his hands. You've seen the X-rays I sent over?'

Anna nodded. 'Yes, and it looks to be a case of simple syndactyly. The second, third and fourth fingers on both hands are fused by soft tissue, but the bones are separate. Let me take a look at him.'

The nurse lifted the baby boy from the cradle, and Anna examined his hands carefully. His fingernails were also fused, but it looked as if separating the fingers would be a relatively straightforward matter.

'This is going to take more than one operation, isn't it?' Jamie was watching her intently, but there was none of their usual joking rivalry in his manner.

'Yes, it's not possible to operate on more than one side of the finger at a time, or there's a risk of damaging the blood supply. When the time comes to operate he's going to need probably four procedures.'

'We'll be sending him up to the ward soon—

is there anything I need to ask them to look out for?'

'I don't see any signs of a more complex syndrome but they should be aware of the possibility. I'll add my recommendations to his notes.'

'Great. Thanks. Can I leave you to it for a moment? I'll be right back…' As usual, Jamie had more than one patient to attend to.

'Yes, that's fine. I'll watch him.'

Both Jamie and the nurse hurried out of the cubicle. The little boy began to fret in his cradle, and Anna couldn't resist picking him up to soothe him.

She wouldn't…couldn't have her own child. The nieces and nephews she'd gained when she'd married had never really belonged to her and, along with their parents, had just melted away again after the divorce. And this little one was only hers for a few short moments, before Jamie or the nurse returned. But he didn't know that, all he knew was the reassurance of being held by someone.

'Hey there, sweetheart. Everything's going to be all right.' She cooed the words at him, and he seemed to respond to her voice.

Everything was very far from being all right.

An abandoned baby who faced painful medical procedures. It seemed such a cruel twist of fate when Anna would have done anything to have her own child. She felt tears well in her eyes, and blinked them away quickly.

She rocked the baby boy in her arms, singing to him quietly, and his eyes began to close. He was so peacefully unaware of everything that was going on around him.

She could put him back into his cradle, now, but somehow it seemed wrong to do so, as if holding him might add just a drop more love to a life that already needed all the love it could get. When Jamie returned, she was still holding the little boy, the notes untouched. He glanced at them and then looked at her.

'Everything okay?'

'Oh. Yes…'

Jamie finally managed a smile. 'They smell so good, don't they? My sister always had a battle on her hands, getting me to hand her newborns back…'

He shot her a speculative look and when Anna failed to answer he seemed to decide that he needed to delve a little further. 'This little man tugs at the heartstrings.'

Anna's heartstrings were close to snapping. And she'd forgotten to really take in that new baby smell. It was too late now, and it was just one more loss to contend with.

'What's his name?' She asked the question before she'd really thought about it, and Jamie shook his head slowly. Of course. They didn't know.

'He'll be staying here for a little while, while his foster care is arranged. I dare say the nurses upstairs will be giving him a name.'

He took the baby from her arms, and Anna tried not to notice the way his face softened. Jamie's green eyes seemed to be cutting into her heart more painfully than usual. He put the baby back into the cradle, stopping to gently stroke his cheek with one finger.

'I really appreciate your time, thank you.'

'No problem. I'll just write my recommendations up and then I'll be on my way.' Anna decided that everything would go a bit faster if she did them outside, where she couldn't be distracted by either Jamie or the baby. She picked up the notes and headed for the door of the cubicle.

'Anna…' Jamie's voice behind her sounded suddenly strained.

'Yes?'

'How is he?'

There was no need to ask who he was talking about. Jamie wasn't as unconcerned about his brother as he seemed.

'He's fine, Jamie. I saw him this morning and he's settling in well.'

Jamie nodded. 'Thanks.'

Nothing else. No indication that Jamie would come to see his brother, and no message. But she'd done all she could and it was time to take a step back now, and let Jamie work things out. And she did have to get back to the clinic.

Anna turned, getting the distinct impression that Jamie was watching her as she walked away.

Five o'clock. She should be going home, but Jon hadn't had a visitor all day. Anna decided to pop in and see how he was, but when she looked in his room he wasn't there. She found him up on the roof of the building, huddled in a heavy leather jacket and a scarf. As she walked towards him, he slid the headphones he was wearing down around his neck.

'Aren't you cold?' An autumn chill was beginning to set in and the evenings were drawing in.

'Nah, I'm good. I like it up here.' Jon tapped his finger on the book in his lap. 'I have plenty of company.'

Music and books. They were wonderful company but didn't replace a family. Anna wondered where Jamie was, and what he was doing.

'You contacted him, didn't you?' Jon was looking at her keenly.

'Yes, I did. I went over to the hospital yesterday and saw him.' Anna bit her lip. Maybe she shouldn't have let Jon know that Jamie was so close, or that it had been more than twenty-four hours since Jamie had heard that his brother was here. But Jon just nodded.

'I'm not gonna ask you what he said.' Jon shifted fitfully in his seat. 'You think we're alike?'

The question came right out of the blue, and it was a difficult one. The two brothers looked alike, but… Jamie was Jamie. He was unique.

'You resemble each other. You seem different to me.'

Jon laughed suddenly. 'Good answer. We used to hate it when we were kids and people reckoned we were just two versions of the same. We had this aunt who always bought identical Christmas presents for us, even when I was on the road, touring, and Jamie was at medical school.'

There was regret in Jon's face. He obviously missed his brother, and Anna wondered again what had torn them apart. Neither of them seemed to want to talk about it, and in that they were identical.

'I guess that's one of the hazards of being a twin.'

'Yeah. Jamie was always the one who said less but had more going on in his head.'

Anna smiled. 'I can't imagine that the person who wrote "Everywhere" doesn't have something going on in his head.'

'You like that song?'

'Yes, I love it. It got me through a bit of a rocky patch in my life. It's so...optimistic about the future.'

'It's a great song.' Jon's lip quivered. 'Jamie

wrote it, you know. I imagine he probably hasn't told you that.'

'No, he didn't.'

'Like I said. Jamie has a lot more going on in his head than I do. I generally used to write the music and he wrote the words, but "Everywhere" was all his own work.'

They must have been close once. If writing songs together wasn't proof enough, then she had only to look at the regret in Jon's face. Maybe she should change the subject, even if the words to 'Everywhere' were now running insistently through her head. The hope for the future and the determination not to give up made so much more sense now that she knew they were Jamie's words.

'What are you listening to?'

Jon took the headphones from around his neck, detaching the earpieces from their mounting and handing one to her. She pressed it against her ear, leaning forward so that Jon could listen through the other one, and he traced his thumb across the screen of the phone he'd taken out of his pocket.

'Bach! Really…?'

Jon laughed. 'Both Jamie and I had music

lessons when we were kids and we played all the classics. Bach was always my favourite. Don't you think this has a lot in common with all song structures?'

'Now you mention it, I suppose…' Anna put the earpiece against her ear again, and Jon began to trace the precise tempo with his finger in the air, like a conductor. When the complex strands of the melody wove together to draw the music to a close, he made a concluding flourish and Anna laughed.

'I see it now…' Anna looked over her shoulder as Jon's gaze suddenly left her face. Jamie was standing by the door that led from the stairs to the roof garden, watching them.

Something about the look on Jamie's face made her quickly give the earpiece back to Jon and lean away from him. She was just talking to a patient, wasn't she? Maybe Jamie thought that she was taking sides, because he shot her an injured look.

'Jon, I…' She turned back to Jon, whose face was moulded into a look of stony shock. 'I didn't know he was coming.'

Jon didn't reply. His attention was all on Jamie, who was walking towards them, and the closer his brother got, the more agitated Jon looked. This whole situation was turning into a nightmare. Something was about to explode…

'I heard you were here.' Jamie's voice was quiet, his face impassive.

'Yeah. I'm here.'

Jamie sat down, without even looking at Anna. The two brothers regarded each other steadily. It would be good to leave right now, but Anna wasn't going anywhere until she knew that they weren't going to start arguing as soon as she turned her back.

'Let's take a look at your arm, little brother.'

Jamie's quiet words seemed familiar to Jon, and he gave a stiff smile as he pulled up the sleeve of his jacket to expose the bottom half of the burn scar. Jamie turned the edges of his mouth down.

'Looks as if it hurt. Probably still does.'

'Yeah. The doc says she can sort it for me.'

Jamie nodded, turning to Anna with the hint of a smile. 'You don't mind if I step on your toes?'

He'd never asked before, but then they'd never been in this situation before. She stood, flashing a smile at Jon. 'I'll leave you to it, if that's okay.'

Jon nodded, and Jamie turned his attention again to his brother. When Anna reached the door that led to the staircase, she turned and saw him examining the scar on Jon's arm carefully. Then he gestured towards his brother's face, and Jon turned his head so that Jamie could see the scars on his brow and neck.

She shouldn't stay. But her heart was beating like a drum in her chest. One spark and the fragile reconciliation could all go up in smoke. Jamie and Jon were talking, and Jamie gestured to the book on Jon's lap. Jon picked it up and began to read aloud, and Jamie leaned back in his chair.

That was an odd thing to do. But it seemed to be part of an old bond that she knew nothing about, and the taut lines of Jamie's body began to relax a little. As they did so, Jon began to smile. Anna shook her head. Whatever worked for them. She turned, opening the door. One last look told her that neither of the brothers was even aware that she was leaving.

CHAPTER THREE

HARD? THIS HAD been much more than hard. More than any of the adjectives that Jamie could apply to any given situation. But he'd known he had to come, and when he'd shrugged on his jacket and left the hospital it hadn't even occurred to him to call ahead. He just wanted to see Jon, and make sure that he was all right.

The receptionist in the ward knew him, but she gave him a second look when he asked for Jon, as if she'd only just noticed the resemblance and put the two names together. It had been a long time since anyone had asked whether he and Jon were related, and Jamie guessed it was because their lives were so very different.

He'd reached the top of the stairs and stopped short, shock gluing him to the spot. Anna was leaning towards Jon and they were both listening to the same piece of music. He always noticed everything about Anna, and now he saw that her blonde hair, usually tied back when she was working, was loose and falling forward across her shoulders. Just inches from Jon's hand.

The intimacy was obvious, and he wanted to grab Anna and pull her away. But Anna wasn't his to protect, and she had every right to spend time with Jon if she wanted to. Then Jon saw him, and the two started almost guiltily.

Rage flowed through him like a tide of molten lava. He couldn't do this. He couldn't see Anna with Jon. But he somehow managed to get himself under control and walked towards them.

An hour later, he'd brought Jon back down to his room, and bade him goodnight. His head was spinning, and he didn't want to see Anna. But his legs didn't obey the command of his head, and he walked towards her office, knowing he'd find her there.

'You're still here?' He stood at the open door, trying to feign surprise.

'Yes. I've been trying to make up my mind about whether I did the right thing or not. And wondering if there was going to be an explosion…' She gave him a nervous smile.

'No explosions. You did the right thing.'

She nodded. 'Come in. I'll get you some coffee.'

Jamie walked into the office, sitting down in the chair on the other side of her desk. 'No coffee. I don't think I'll be sleeping much tonight as it is.'

'I'm glad you've patched things up. Whatever this argument was about…' She waved her hand, as if that didn't matter.

She didn't know. Jamie told himself that it made the intimacy he'd seen between Anna and his brother a little less shattering, but he still couldn't put it out of his mind. He reminded himself that he'd seen Anna many times with patients, and that her manner was always caring and kind. He should look at it in that context.

'We haven't so much patched it up as… We're not talking about it.'

Anna shrugged. 'Whatever works…'

Who knew whether it was going to work or not? Right now it was about the only option as Jamie still couldn't talk about what had happened without betraying his anger, and right now Jon needed his care.

'Do the rest of the family know Jon's here?' There were a lot of questions he hadn't asked Jon, and Jamie realised that he'd been saving them for Anna.

'Not as far as I'm aware. Jon said that if you weren't coming then he didn't want the rest of the family to have to take sides.'

'That was decent of him. Unnecessary, though. I'll call my sister tonight. My parents are in Australia for three months, but I'll email them and let them know.'

'Sounds like a plan.' Anna's obvious approval began to cut through the haze of uncertainty that Jamie felt. 'You'll be back?'

'Tomorrow morning. The charity can do without me for a couple of weeks, and I'll be staying up in London full time.'

Anna nodded. Another little shard of warmth, something concrete to hold onto.

'If you'd like, you can use my office to work in while you're here. I'll mention it to my boss but I doubt he'll have any problem with the idea. You work with us on an informal basis anyway.'

'You're keeping me here for as long as you can?' Jamie flashed her a smile.

'That's the general idea.' She smiled back. Honesty was one of Anna's more endearing traits.

'Thanks. That would be really helpful and… I should spend as much time as I can with Jon, but it would be nice to have a bolthole as well.'

'I thought that might be the case.' Anna leaned back in her chair, regarding him thoughtfully. 'So what's with the reading?'

She didn't know *that* either. It was no secret, but Jamie's habit was to compensate for his dyslexia as much as possible when he was working. 'I have mild dyslexia. When we were kids, Jon used to read to me. It was usually comics then, he used to do different voices and act things out.'

'Ah. So that explains the planner on your office wall, then.' She smiled at him. 'And your diary. I thought you were just terrifyingly organised.'

Both his diary and his calendar were colour coded, allowing Jamie to see what was most important at a glance. It was one of the many small techniques he employed that most people didn't even notice, even if they knew about his dyslexia.

'Yeah, I find that colour coding makes things a bit easier. Although I wouldn't want to dissuade you from your belief in my organisational skills.'

'Okay. I'll remain suitably terrified.' She shot him a smile. 'Jon says that you both made music together when you were young as well.'

Jamie knew exactly what Anna was doing. She was gently probing, getting him to talk in much the same way as she got all her patients and their families to. Soon he'd find himself tempted to tell her about his darkest fears, the way they did.

He'd meet that problem when he came to it. Jamie wondered if Anna knew that he'd been concentrating on the things they'd shared before the bust-up as a way of reconnecting with his brother, and decided that she'd probably already worked that out.

'Yeah. He was always the showman, though. The one who liked to get up and sing.'

'He told me that you wrote "Everywhere". It's one of my favourite songs.'

Her smile made his heart beat a little faster.

Maybe Anna had let his words into her life, as she'd sung along to them on the radio… The thought made his hand tremble.

'I…um…was at a bit of a turning point in my life when I wrote it. I'd applied to medical school and they'd accepted me, despite the dyslexia. It was a dream I never thought I'd be able to accomplish, but I was also a bit concerned about how I might cope.'

Anna nodded her head. 'That's what I like about the song. It seems to me to be all about hope and accomplishing your dreams. Maybe not in the way you thought you would, but doing it anyway. Suddenly your charity makes a lot more sense.'

Jamie dragged his thoughts from wondering where she'd first heard 'Everywhere' and what she'd been doing, and focussed his mind on his charity. That usually gave him a bit of clarity.

'The charity only exists because of the royalties from the song.'

'And you and Jon did that together.' She gave a little nod of approval.

Much as he liked the feeling of having made a connection with Anna, Jamie couldn't think about it any more. In retrospect, 'Everywhere' had been the beginning of the end for him and Jon. It had blasted his brother into the stratosphere of fame and set their paths on an ever-diverging trajectory.

'Yeah, look… I'd like to see Jon's notes.'

Anna pursed her lips. Maybe she was about to give him the lecture about stepping on her toes and leaving her to get on with treating her own patients. Jamie flashed her an apologetic look.

'You're asking as a doctor? Or as his brother?'

That was the nub of it. Jamie had always imagined himself a doctor first, beyond anything. 'His brother.'

'Fair enough. I'll have to check with Jon first, of course.'

'Of course.'

'Right, then.' Anna got to her feet, and Jamie took the hint. He should be going now. But when he started to rise from his seat she waved him back down again. 'Stay there. I won't be a minute.'

She was actually a little more than a minute. Jamie stared at the wall, trying to rearrange his thoughts, but everything seemed jumbled, like words on a page that wouldn't respond to any of his normal reading techniques. He was out of his depth, and the old panic about whether he'd be able to make sense of anything had returned. And he was hanging on to Anna for dear life.

He wondered if the families of her other patients felt like this. That she could be trusted to steer them through the myriad of decisions that faced them, all of which seemed frighteningly incomprehensible. He guessed they probably did…

'All right.' Anna bustled back into the room, making him jump. 'I've spoken to Jon and he was very pleased you were taking an interest. My only reservation is that you remember who you are…'

'You're his surgeon, Anna. I'm a concerned family member, who happens to understand the issues involved a little better.'

'Perfect. In that case, we could go for coffee and something to eat if you like. I skipped lunch…'

He hadn't eaten either. Jamie wondered if her reasons were the same as his, and let it go. And suddenly he found himself at a loose end. He wouldn't be driving back down to Hastings tonight—after all, his place was here with Jon, and he'd stay in his London bedsit for as long as it took.

'That sounds great.'

He followed her out of the building, and she crossed the road, obviously making for somewhere. Jamie didn't much care where.

'Italian okay for you? They do food upstairs in the evenings, and it's pretty quiet around this time.' She led him through winding back streets to a bustling coffee bar.

'Yeah. Anything…'

Anna nodded. Upstairs the restaurant area was quiet, just a few evening diners, and she led him to one of the booths that lined the far wall, which afforded them some privacy. Jamie managed to remember to help her out of her coat and lay it down on the bench that ran around the table.

A waiter approached them, wearing a smile and handing Jamie two menus. He passed one to Anna and fixed his gaze onto his own.

The closely typed words seemed to be moving in front of him, locked in a complicated dance, and not heeding his silent exhortations to just sit back down in their usual places and behave. Tonight they were breaking free of the framework he usually applied and continuing with their hedonistic movement.

'Mmm…' Anna was studying her menu. 'Lasagne looks nice… Or tagliatelle. They do a really nice carbonara here, but I think I'm a bit hungrier than that…'

Was she reading the menu to him? Jamie decided that he didn't care if she was. So what if he could usually manage without betraying his difficulties. This evening, he was too stressed out to use his usual coping strategies.

'I think I'll have the carbonara.'

She nodded. 'Yes, I think I will too. We can always have a second course. Are we having wine?'

'Don't let me stop you. I'll stick to water.'

'Okay.' She closed the menu decisively and beckoned to the waiter.

Jamie was obviously struggling. Whatever the argument between him and his brother had been about, it must have been bad. Something life-changing that had parted brothers who had once been close. Since it was clear that neither of them were going to talk about it, Anna had to quell her curiosity and just hope that they could work it out between themselves. The way that Jamie had responded to the knowledge that Jon was in hospital made it quite clear that he *wanted* to work it out.

And he'd written 'Everywhere'. The song that gave people hope. In the dark days after her marriage had ended so abruptly, she'd sung it at the top of her voice, along with all the other survival songs in her break-up playlist.

And now she had to get Jamie through tonight. She could see him eyeing the folder that was sticking out of the top of her handbag, and when the waiter brought her a glass of white wine, she took a mouthful and gave Jamie his brother's medical records.

He opened the folder, running his finger under the printed words. She'd seen him do that before and had thought little of it. But he seemed to be struggling rather more than usual, probably because of the stress he was under.

'This doesn't make any sense.' He wiped his hand across his face. 'Or is it just me…?'

'No, it's not you. When Jon first came to the clinic he made an outpatient appointment with

Dr Lewis—he just said that he was away from home and needed general medical advice. He asked primarily about the burns, but he also complained of a whole raft of other unconnected symptoms and Dr Lewis suspected that there were other underlying issues. He told Jon that he wanted to give him a more thorough assessment, which Jon agreed to, so he was booked into the clinic, and referred to me for scar revision.'

'Right. You're saying he has something else wrong with him?'

'We found out that he'd been in hospital in America about six weeks ago. There's a summary of the notes that they sent through on the next page.' Anna reminded herself of Dr Lewis's advice to her this morning. Tread carefully. Answer questions and let both Jamie and Jon take things at their own pace.

Jamie turned the page, running his finger along the printed lines. It stopped at the list of medications that Jon been prescribed. 'These are strong anti-depressants. What aren't you telling me? And why on earth didn't you tell me before?'

That was an unequivocal expression of intent. Jamie wanted to know everything. Anna took another sip from her glass, resisting the impulse to gulp the lot down.

'Second question first, I didn't tell you before now because I didn't have permission to do so. It's up to Jon whether you see his medical records or not. So you can thank him for letting me show you this when you see him tomorrow.'

'Okay. That put me in my place.' The signs of strain were showing on Jamie's face, and Anna longed to reach out and touch him.

'I have to do everything properly, Jamie. You must understand that.'

He nodded, taking a sip of water. Jamie knew all this, but he was asking the same things that any concerned family member would. 'Okay. And my first question?'

'I don't have a final answer to that, yet. We've talked to Jon about his previous stay in hospital, and all he says is that he just lost it for a while. Apparently he'd locked himself in his hotel room and wouldn't come out, and everyone just left him there for two days, until the hotel staff raised the alarm. We know that he's exhausted and very probably depressed, but we have to rule out any physical causes for his symptoms.'

Jamie nodded his head, flipping the pages and reading through the rest of the file. 'So you're still in the diagnosis stage at the moment. What does Jon say about that?'

Anna shrugged. 'We've explained everything to him, and he just tells us to go ahead and do whatever we want. He doesn't seem to care. He says he wants to stay and get the burns sorted out, but my opinion is that the clinic is a safe place for him at the moment. A refuge.'

Jamie heaved a sigh. The pain in his eyes was almost tearing Anna's heart out. 'He didn't want me to know, did he? Everything was falling to pieces, and he didn't want me to know…'

Anna had come to the same conclusion, and glossed over it for Jamie's sake. 'Maybe he thought you wouldn't come. But he was wrong about that, wasn't he?'

'I took my time.' He shot her an anguished look.

'You came. That's all that matters. Don't beat yourself up about it, there are plenty of more constructive things you can do with your time right now.'

He pinched the bridge of his nose with two fingers, shaking his head as if he were trying to clear it. 'That's your standard advice, is it?'

There was a trace of the confrontation that seasoned any discussion they had about a patient. But this time it was bitter, with no hint of a smile.

'I may have said it a few times before. That doesn't mean it isn't true, Jamie. I don't underestimate my patients' families. Did you think for one minute I'd say anything different to you because you're a doctor?'

For one moment she was lost in his gaze. Those searching eyes that seemed to need so much from her at the moment. Then he smiled.

'You really *are* trying to put me in my place, aren't you?'

'There's nothing wrong with knowing your boundaries, in any particular situation. Being a great doctor isn't going to help you now. Jon needs you as a brother. I know that's difficult for you, on lots of different levels.'

He nodded. 'All that matters at the moment is that he needs me. So I should remember to eat and sleep, and just be there for him. Because concentrating on his medical care is just my way of distancing myself from the emotional issues.'

'Yeah. You're getting it now.' Jamie always had been aware of what his patients and their families went through emotionally, and now he got to put that knowledge into practice.

He smiled, that same smile that he always wore when she'd prevailed in one of their debates. Jamie could never be accused of being a sore loser.

'Thanks, Anna. I really appreciate what you've done here.'

She could feel herself beginning to blush, the way she always did when Jamie spared some praise for her. She took a gulp of wine, hoping the gesture might cover her pleasure, or at least explain the redness of her cheeks.

'No problem. All part of the service.' That was an obfuscation too. Anna had longed for brothers and sisters when she had been growing up, and then she'd found a family and lost them again. Losing each other must have been ten times harder for Jamie and Jon. She'd go to any lengths to make sure that the fragile reconciliation between them took root and flourished.

CHAPTER FOUR

'I DON'T LIKE sleeping here.'

Nine-year-old Darren greeted Anna and Jamie with a frown. Jamie had been at the clinic all day yesterday, and had arrived at the crack of dawn this morning, and Anna had given in to the inevitable and asked him to come with her to see Darren. He'd been working with the boy and his family for the last two years, ever since Darren had been scalded by hot water. The long process of medical care and counselling had been successful, but the skin graft on the boy's leg had failed and Jamie had arranged for it to be replaced here.

'No?' Jamie sat down beside the boy's bed. 'Why not?'

'This place stinks. And my leg hurts. I want to go home.'

'All right. The thing is, I don't think your leg's going to hurt any less at home.'

Darren rolled his eyes. 'I don't like it here.'

'Your mum will be here soon. Will that make you feel a bit better?'

'No. They're only going to go home again, and I'll be on my own.'

Jamie considered the matter carefully. Anna liked the way he always took the youngsters in his care at their word, listening carefully to their concerns and never dismissing them.

'You've got a point. So if I tell you that I'll do something about that, will you let Anna take a look at your skin graft?'

'You *have* to do something.' Darren was obviously upset, and he wasn't going to let this go.

'I'll sort things out. You have my word on that.'

Jamie's word was clearly enough for Darren. That kind of trust took a lot of work to build, and Anna watched as Jamie took his phone out of his pocket, handing it over to the boy. He brightened instantly.

'You've got the new game!'

'Yeah, I thought you'd like it. You can show me how to play it.'

Darren was losing no time. As Anna carefully removed the outer dressings on his leg and examined the skin graft, he was already tapping on Jamie's phone, wrinkling his nose when something went wrong.

'Darren, stay still for me…' The boy nodded in response to Anna, his concentration on the phone. Her observations told her that the graft she'd transplanted the day before was in good condition.

'That looks really good, Darren…' Jamie had to nudge him before he responded. When he did, he gave Anna one of the bright smiles that he'd given her yesterday.

'Thank you, Anna.'

'You're very welcome. Now I want you to do something for me.'

She leaned towards him, and Darren momentarily lost interest in the phone. It slid from his fingers, and Jamie caught it before it fell onto the floor.

'I've got some things to do now.' Nothing was as important as Darren at the moment, but she would find something to occupy her time. 'Jamie's going to ask you what we can do to make you feel a bit happier here. I want you to tell him, because I really want you to be happy.'

Darren nodded, and Anna glanced at Jamie. She'd relied on him before to talk to their young patients, and find out what was bothering them, but this time there was no trace of the customary adversarial looks that flashed between them. Just warmth. A warmth that made her heart beat a little faster and tingles run down her spine.

'And Anna will sort everything out for you.' Jamie flashed her a delicious smile.

'Will you make me a list?' Anna tore a piece of paper from the notepad that she carried with her, and laid it on the bed. 'Maybe different colours…?'

'That sounds like a plan. We'll colour code it, shall we? Red for the things you really don't like, eh?' Jamie took a red pen from his pocket. 'We'll do those first.'

Anna wasn't sure what to expect when she made her way back to Darren's room. But the boy seemed cheerful and Jamie rose, patting his pocket and giving him a conspiratorial smile. Leaving him to play with his phone, he ushered Anna outside.

'All right. Let's have it.' She held out her hand, and Jamie gave her the folded paper.

'It's… This is what he said.'

The paper was divided into three. At the top, written in red, were the things that were really bothering Darren. Anna scanned Jamie's neat, clear handwriting.

'Custard. Okay that's easy enough. No more custard.' Anna read the next entry and frowned. 'Really? There's a ghost in his room…?'

'That's what he said.'

And that was what Jamie had written down. Of course he had, he always took what his young charges said seriously.

'Well…' Anna decided to play along. 'What *kind* of ghost exactly?'

'He says it's a sparkly white woman. She appeared by the television at midnight. He checked the time.'

'And the TV wasn't on? Maybe it had been on standby.'

Jamie shook his head. 'Nope. I asked him that, and he said it wasn't *on* the TV, it was in front of it.

'Midnight. Well, perhaps it was one of the nurses. Darren was recovering from surgery, and he may well have been disoriented or drowsy…' Anna shrugged.

'I mentioned that too and he told me he knows the difference between a nurse and a ghost.' Jamie grinned. 'I imagine that ghosts don't bring you custard and expect you to eat it.'

'No, I imagine they don't.' Anna put her mind to the problem. 'Well, we have another room that's empty at the moment. If it makes Darren feel better then he can move to that one. And we can arrange for an extra bed if his mum would like to stay with him overnight.'

Jamie nodded. 'That would be great. His mum's on her own and has younger children, but she has a sister who helps out. I can arrange for one of our outreach workers to go and stay with them if her sister can't manage.'

'Okay. We'll do that, then. Anything else, apart from the custard? Does his leg hurt him?'

Jamie smiled, pointing to the green list at the bottom of the page. 'It hurts a bit but he says it's okay. I took the liberty of checking…'

Of course he had. But it felt less like a liberty

and more like a helping hand. 'That's great, thanks.'

Anna scanned the rest of the list. Nothing there, apart from the usual dislikes that everyone had of hospitals. 'Perhaps you'd like to take Darren up to the roof garden this afternoon if he'd like a breath of fresh air. I think we have some binoculars somewhere, I'll see if I can find them. He might like to do some sightseeing with them.'

'I think he'd like that.' Jamie shot her an uncertain look. It wasn't like him to hesitate before he asked for something for one of his patients. 'Are you…? Is someone going to be in Darren's old room tonight?'

'I doubt it, there are no new patients coming in today. We're not going to fill it with garlic and brick up the door, though.'

'Garlic's for vampires.' Jamie grinned suddenly. 'They're entirely different. If I've learned anything thing from Darren's games, it's that you need to be armed with the right weapon when you face any given opponent.'

'Well, whatever the right weapon is, we're not going to be using it. Darren's a little boy in a strange place who thought he saw something.'

'He told me exactly what he saw. More than once.'

Anna puffed out a breath. She knew what Jamie was doing, and it was the right thing. He was listening to the most vulnerable person first, and believing what they said.

'Jamie, you can go and look around the new room with him, and check it out. We need to do everything we can to put Darren's mind at rest and help him to heal, but there's no ghost. It's all very well to believe what he says, but there has to be some filter of whether it's actually credible or not.'

Jamie gave her a reproachful look. If he could just wear contacts or dark glasses it might help. His moss-green eyes spoke to her on a level she couldn't resist.

'I filtered. I still can't work out what he saw. You don't believe in ghosts, then?'

Anna shrugged. 'I like to think I have an open mind. That doesn't mean I won't look for an explanation for something I don't understand. And you've got too much time on your hands. If you want something useful to do, you can help us move him.'

Darren's mother arrived, and Jamie took her down to the coffee lounge to explain everything to her. Once she'd approved the plan, the new room was made ready for Darren. His things were gathered together, and then Jamie lifted him out of his bed, carrying him across the central nurses' area, his mother walking alongside.

Anna swallowed hard. The thing Darren most needed right now was love and care, and Jamie was giving him just that. He'd make a great dad. And she suspected that making babies with him would be an ultimate pleasure. One that she'd never enjoy. She turned her back, hurrying away.

'Everything okay?' Anna had spent the evening in her office, doing a few jobs that could have waited. The ward was quiet now, and in darkness.

'Yes, Darren settled down to sleep and his mum's with him.' The nurse gestured towards the closed door of Darren's new room. Anna nodded, turning her gaze towards the half-open door of the room he'd occupied last night.

'Is he there?'

The nurse grinned and nodded. Anna walked towards the door, slipping inside the darkened room.

'So you decided to try your hand at ghost-hunting, did you? Or do you just have nothing better to do on a Friday night?'

Jamie's smile was traced by light, filtering in from outside. Intimate in the shadows. Like the smile of a lover in the half-light.

'I could ask you the same questions.' He murmured.

Anna wasn't going to answer either of them. Particularly the one about having better things to do on a Friday night because she didn't. She spent more evenings here than she liked to admit, and the clinic often felt more like home than her flat did.

'You're not going to stay here all night, are you?' She wouldn't put it past him. Jamie's unswerving belief that Darren *had* seen something, and his determination to find out what, was mesmeric. Attractive in a way that moved her beyond any physical thrill.

'It's gone half eleven. I'm just curious, I'll give it another hour and then I'll go.'

'And you're absolutely sure that it wasn't one of the nurses that Darren saw?' Anna had privately made up her mind that that was the most likely explanation.

'He told me twelve o'clock. The nurses make their rounds on the half hour and I checked the notes for last night. The nurse on duty wrote down when she'd checked on him.'

'This is crazy, Jamie.'

'Yeah, okay. I'll see you tomorrow, then.'

He was calling her bluff. Jamie had slid a long bench across from under the window, and placed it as close as he could to the side of the bed, so that he'd get the same view of the room that Darren would have done last night. Anna sat down beside him, and they lapsed into companionable silence together for a few moments. The temptation to sink into the darkness with him was almost unbearable.

'I heard there was an impromptu concert on the roof this afternoon. Jonny Campbell unplugged.'

She heard Jamie chuckle quietly. 'Yeah, I fetched a guitar from home for him, and asked if he'd like to play. It was a sell-out, we had a crowd of more than a dozen when the nurses' shift changed.'

'Not quite what Jon's used to, then?'

'It was a lot better than he's been used to recently. Jon's been talking about getting back to his roots, and he was enjoying it as much as Darren was. I think it meant something to him. Darren's a brave kid, and making him smile helped Jon, too.'

'It sounds like great therapy. For both of them.' There were some things that the hospital couldn't give to its patients, and this was one of them.

'Darren's mum was pretty thrilled as well. Jon sang "Everywhere" for her, and I took some pictures.'

'You didn't join in?'

'Nah. We're not quite there yet.'

Making music together had been such a bond for Jamie and Jon. Maybe it was too much to expect of their fragile new relationship. 'Next time maybe.'

'Maybe.'

She wanted so badly to touch him, to comfort him. Jamie had put all his own feelings aside and had turned his attention to helping Jon and Darren. He was making a great job of it for both of them, but at some point he was going to have to confront his own emotions. Anna moved her hand, laying it on Jamie's arm in what she hoped would be construed as a friendly gesture of concern.

She felt muscle flex beneath her fingertips. She should move away, but she couldn't. Then she felt Jamie's hand on hers as he leaned towards her. She could hardly breathe.

'It's nearly midnight. Are you frightened yet?' He whispered the words in her ear.

Terrified. Afraid of what might happen if she sat any longer with him in the darkness. The supernatural world had nothing that rivalled this for sheer, unthinking dread.

Then she saw it. A pale figure that seemed to shimmer slightly on the other side of the room. Anna let out a gasp, feeling Jamie's arm move protectively around her shoulders. Suddenly she was clinging to him, feeling the beat of his heart quicken against her cheek. Then he let out a low chuckle.

'So *that's* it.'

* * *

Jamie didn't have an extensive knowledge of ghost-hunting, and had always assumed that it was a ruse, intended to entice a girl closer. If that was the case, then this had unexpectedly worked like a charm. He'd assumed that his night-time vigil would be spent alone, but suddenly Anna had slid towards him and was in his arms.

It was obvious now, what Darren had seen. But his first glimpse of the illusion had taken Jamie by surprise, and he'd automatically reached for Anna, seeking to protect her from the unknown.

'It's…um…a trick of the light.'

'Yes, I can see that.' Anna didn't move away, though.

It was proving extremely difficult to move away from her. The scent of her hair, and the feeling of having her close was driving him crazy. He almost wished that something fearsome and dreadful *had* appeared before them, so he could hold her a little closer.

He drank in the feeling, knowing that it wasn't going to last for long. Then she shifted in his arms and he let her go.

'Had me fooled for a moment, though.' He murmured the words and she nodded.

'Yes. Me too.'

And after that moment the shocked reaction had turned into an embrace. Jamie had wanted to hold her, and it had been very apparent that Anna had wanted it too. The thought was far more disturbing than anything that the night could throw at them.

Jamie got to his feet, walking over to the door, and looking out. He saw it all now. 'It's the night nurse. She's standing at the end of the counter at the nurses' station in front of the work lamp so that she can read the notes before she goes on her rounds.'

'And the light's reflected in the mirror...' Anna gestured towards the full-length mirror that was fixed to the bathroom door.

'And then reflecting again on the screen of the TV...' Jamie moved towards the large screen on the wall at the end of the bed. 'The refraction is giving it an almost 3D quality.'

'But why hasn't anyone seen this before? This room's generally occupied.'

Jamie shrugged. 'Maybe they've moved the work lamp. Or maybe because they left Darren's door open last night to keep an eye on him, and usually the doors are closed.'

The figure disappeared suddenly, and the door was pushed open. The ghost was standing in the doorway, an enquiring look on her face. Anna got to her feet.

'Katya, come and sit over here. We've found our ghost.'

The night nurse looked puzzled, but did as Anna bade her. Jamie decided to stay where he was. The idea of any other woman clinging to him, so soon after he'd felt Anna close, was unthinkable.

He watched Anna walk over to the lamp, and motioned her to the side a little, so that she was standing in exactly the same place that Katya had been. Then he heard a gasp behind him.

'What…! So he *did* see something.'

'Yeah.' Jamie's eyes moved to the blurred figure reflected in the TV screen. This time it seemed a far more alluring ghost. 'Did you move the lamp recently?'

'Yes, we got a new one, and the lead wasn't as long, it won't stretch far enough so we can sit at the desk and read the notes. We were going to ask for an extension cable, but in the meantime I've been standing at the end of the counter…' Katya's hand flew to her mouth. 'Poor little Darren, no wonder he was so upset.'

'Well, at least we've got to the bottom of it now.' Jamie beckoned to Anna, and the form in the TV screen disappeared as she walked back to the doorway.

'I'm so sorry. I thought he was just having nightmares, so I comforted him and sat with him until he went back to sleep.' Katya's mouth turned down. 'I'll move the lamp straight away.'

'You couldn't possibly have foreseen this, none of us did. And don't move the lamp just yet…' Anna flashed a look at Jamie, as if she already knew what he was about to say.

'Yes, I'd like to show this to Darren in the morning. If that's okay.'

'Of course. I might even come and do a turn as the friendly ghost.' Anna's smile seemed luminous in the interplay of light and shade in the doorway, and Jamie wondered if Darren would see it too. A beautiful, friendly ghost. Who seemed intent on picking the pieces of his heart up and stitching them back together. It was complex surgery, and Jamie doubted that even Anna was equal to it. He was too broken, and there would always be a little chink missing that let in the doubts and the mistrust.

But he could still walk Anna back down to her office. Still enjoy her scent, which, now that he'd noticed it, was more intoxicating than he'd ever imagined. And when she turned, flinging her arms around his neck and then retreating away from him almost as quickly, he felt his heart beating in his chest.

'What was that for?'

'Because you believed Darren.' Anna gave a shrug. 'I mean, we all believed that was what he *thought* he saw, and we took it seriously. But you believed him, and you found the answer.'

The warmth of her praise was working its way through him. If it reached his heart he wouldn't be able to stop himself from kissing her. 'I didn't discount the idea that it might have been his imagination.'

'But you waited up, all the same.'

'Oh, and you're not really here?'

She wiggled her fingers and whoo-whooed at him, in a laughing impression of a ghost. 'Maybe. Maybe not...'

'So how are you getting home?' Now that

Jamie had betrayed the protective streak he felt for Anna, he may as well go the whole hog and not just fret about whether she got home safely.

'I'll call a cab. Would you like a lift?'

'I'm only twenty minutes' walk. I could do with the fresh air.'

She made the call, and when the cab arrived, he walked her down to the main reception area and out into the street. Opening the back door of the car for her, he suppressed the impulse to warn the driver that he was carrying precious cargo and stepped back onto the pavement, watching as the cab drew away.

A walk would do him good. The last few days had been all about trying to find something to say to Jon that would encourage him and make him feel better, and ignoring the elephant in the room. But Anna had turned everything that he'd thought he knew on its head, and made anything seem possible.

CHAPTER FIVE

THE SOUND OF raised voices came from Jon's room. Anna supposed it was inevitable as Jamie and Jon couldn't keep ignoring whatever it was that they'd argued about. But when she approached the door, she found that she'd been wrong. They seemed to be managing to ignore it *and* argue at the same time.

'Hello…' Anna pushed the door open a little further. 'Am I interrupting anything?'

They both looked up from the crossword they'd been discussing, and she thought she saw a flash of relief in Jamie's eyes. 'Hi. What are you doing here on a Saturday morning?'

'I was going to help you show Darren his ghost, remember?'

Jamie nodded. 'The ward sister says that I can pull down the shades and try it out after lunch. She's interested as well.'

'So am I,' Jon chimed in. 'Poor little chap, he must have been frightened. Waking up like that and seeing things. I'm glad you managed to explain it for him.'

There was a note of sadness in Jon's voice. Anna wondered what the silent hours of the night had held for him. Demons, maybe, fuelled by exhaustion and depression. She smiled, sitting down opposite Jon.

'How are *you* today?'

Jon shook off his reverie. 'Okay. Thirteen down's giving us a bit of a problem.'

Anna picked up the paper, examining the crossword. 'Humerus.'

'Of course!' Jon took the paper, filling in the word. 'You should have got that one, Jamie. What's the point of medical school if you don't know the name for a clown's arm?'

'Upper arm, technically.' Jamie frowned. His mood seemed to have darkened suddenly. Anna put the folder containing her notes down on the table, and decided she should get down to business.

'I wanted to talk to you about your arm, Jon.' She glanced at Jamie and he gave her a questioning look, then got the message.

'Okay, I'll leave you both to it, then.' He got to his feet.

'Stay.' For a moment there was an imploring look in Jon's eyes, but it was quickly masked. 'You never know, you might learn something.'

Jamie ignored the jibe, and sat down again. 'If that's okay.'

'Yes, of course.' Anna settled the matter as firmly as she could. 'So how is the burn feeling now, Jon?'

'Okay. It doesn't itch so much.'

'Yes, I'm happy with the way that the cream has helped moisturise the skin and take down some of the inflammation.'

'You'll be doing the procedure soon?' Jon's restless anxiety was never far from the surface and he shifted in his seat.

'That's what I'd like to talk to you about. You've already had a couple of sessions with our counsellor, and Dr Lewis has prescribed medication for depression. In view of that, and the fact that you're also very run down, we both think it would be best to postpone any surgery on your arm until we've tackled those important issues.'

Jon frowned. 'My arm's a mess. *Anyone* would be depressed.'

Anna had anticipated some resistance from

Jon, and decided that the most straightforward answers were the best. 'It's normal to have feelings in reaction to an injury. But that's not necessarily the same as depression.'

Jon shook his head. 'I want this done. I want rid of it.'

'Anything we do to modify the scars on your arm and face will make them more painful in the short term—'

'I don't *care* about pain. If it hurts, it hurts. It's not as if everything else is rosy at the moment.'

That was exactly what Anna and Dr Lewis had discussed yesterday. Jon was in a world of mental pain and confusion, and they needed to address that first. The pain from a medical procedure might serve to take his mind off his other problems, but it would do nothing to solve them.

'We feel that these other issues are more pressing and should be addressed first. We'll still keep up with the cream and massage, and that will improve the skin around your burns and make it more likely that surgery will be successful.'

Jon shook his head, cursing under his breath.

Then got to his feet and started to pace. 'This is… Why can't you just do as I say?'

Anna shot Jamie a warning look, hoping he wouldn't intervene, and he ignored her.

'Hey! You think you're the most important person in the room? You're not, Anna is. Because she's your surgeon and you need to listen to what she's telling you and follow her advice.' Jamie's voice was quiet but very firm. And it worked. Jon calmed down suddenly.

'Sorry. I don't much like sitting around, doing nothing.' Jon's moods could turn on a sixpence, and now he seemed the picture of contrition.

'You have nothing to apologise for. I know it must be hard, and frustrating, but both Dr Lewis and I feel that this is the best way forward. If you agree, he'll take over sole responsibility for your care for the foreseeable future, and you can come back to me when you've worked together to resolve the most important issues.'

Jon shrugged. 'Okay, whatever you say. Although I'll miss my beautiful Anna's visits.'

Anna saw Jamie stiffen, and felt herself blush. It was just a compliment and it meant nothing to her. It would have meant a great deal more on Jamie's lips…

'It's not a beauty contest, mate.' Jamie's tension showed beneath his smile. 'Anna's here to do her job.'

He was right, but he hadn't needed to say it. Jon's words were harmless.

'I'll always take a compliment.' She tried to diffuse the tension that had built suddenly in the room.

Jon chuckled, and Jamie looked at her as if she'd just slapped his face. Whatever was going on between them was one of the things that needed to be resolved. A knock sounded at the door and Anna jumped to her feet to open it.

A woman of about her own age was juggling a baby and a large bag. Her resemblance to Jamie and Jon was obvious.

'Look who it is! Is that Joshua…?' Jon was animated again, and even Jamie looked a little less grumpy.

'Yes, I thought you might like to get to know your new nephew.' The woman turned to Anna. 'I'm Caroline, Jamie and Jon's sister.'

'I'm Anna Caulder. I was Jon's surgeon until about five minutes ago.'

'Jamie's told me all about you. Thanks for looking after my big brothers.' Caroline grinned, clearly reckoning that *both* of her brothers had needed some looking after. 'And this is Joshua.'

'Hey, Joshua.' Jon's voice was cracked with emotion and he was staring at Caroline and the baby. Caroline planted a kiss on her son's brow and pointed towards Jon, waving at him. Joshua imitated his mother, and Jon waved back.

'Don't let me interrupt…' Caroline smiled at Anna, and Anna shook her head. This was exactly what Jon needed.

'We're finished. I'll leave you to your visit.' Anna shot Jamie a pointed look and he got to his feet. Despite his obvious annoyance, he too understood that Caroline and Jon needed some time together, and that baby Joshua was a very special visitor too.

Jamie ushered his sister to a seat then followed Anna out of the room. She closed the door and Jamie paused, looking at her thoughtfully.

'Is there something *you* need to talk about?' Strictly speaking, and now that she was no longer Jon's surgeon, that was Dr Lewis's question to ask. But Jamie was a friend.

'Yeah, actually, there is.' She saw a trace of annoyance in his eyes.

'Right, then.' She turned on her heel, beckoning to him over her shoulder. 'My office.'

Anna walked into her office, perching herself on the windowsill and folding her arms. 'All right. What gives?'

She was going to push it. Right now probably wasn't the time.

'Nothing…'

'Don't *nothing* me, Jamie. You've been swallowing something for days, and it's got something to do with me and the way I've been treating your brother. So let's have it.'

'You've done everything right. I think that the decision to have Dr Lewis take over is an excellent one.' Jamie decided that the best course was the least antagonistic one.

'And…?'

Okay. If she wanted to know so much… Maybe it was something that he should have mentioned to her before. Sitting down would be good, it might make him feel less angry, but somehow being confined in a seat was unthinkable.

'I think… Jon's very charming. Charismatic…'

'And…?'

Jamie puffed out a breath. 'Don't be fooled by it. He just loves the attention and he's broken a few hearts.' *His* heart. Jon had broken his heart as well. Jamie swallowed down the thought.

A slight flush spread across her cheeks and as it did so, Jamie's stomach did a somersault. Not Anna. He couldn't bear to think that she might have fallen prey to Jon's charm.

'You think that I haven't been professional?'

'No, but now that you're no longer his surgeon, that's not an issue, is it?' Jamie shook his head. 'This is just…friendly advice.'

Anna's eyebrows shot up. 'Friendly advice? You think I need *friendly advice* to keep my hands off the patients?'

She was angry now, and deliberately misunderstanding him. Jamie felt his own anger begin to bubble furiously.

'No, of course not, we both know how to

act professionally. But I've seen how you look at him, the way you were listening to music together up on the roof the other evening...' Jamie couldn't even think about it.

'How *dare* you?' She marched across the room, stopping just inches in front of him, her face suddenly cold with rage.

'Anna, I'm not suggesting you've done anything wrong. I just don't want to see you getting hurt.'

'No, Jamie. You're telling me that I've been inappropriate with a patient. I found him sitting up there on the roof on his own, and I took a moment to talk to him. You understand *talking*, don't you? If you saw a reaction from me when you arrived, maybe it was because you were looking daggers at me.'

Her indignant fury left no room for doubt. He'd allowed his own feelings for Anna to get in the way of his judgement, and he'd jumped to the conclusion that had been presented to him by his own relationship with his brother. Jamie suddenly felt very ashamed of himself.

'Do I get to apologise?' Maybe she didn't want to hear it. Not after what he'd said.

'Damn right you get to apologise. I'm not

entirely sure how much good it'll do, though.' Anna's face had softened a little as she threw down the challenge.

Jamie took a breath. He had to make this good. 'Then I apologise. Unreservedly. I was wrong to suggest that your motives were anything other than kindness. And you're right, my reaction was nothing to do with you, and everything to do with me. I've been trying not to lash out at Jon, and I lashed out at you instead. I'm sorry.'

He could feel the tension in the room lifting. He wanted to hug her, but he didn't dare. In the silence between them, he felt himself begin to shake with emotion.

'That's a very nice apology. And it's accepted.' Anna moved her hand, brushing her fingers against his trembling hand, and he felt desire flood through him. No. She was just being a kind friend. He wasn't going to mistake that for something else, not so soon after he'd made such a similar, horrendous mistake.

'Thank you. I don't really deserve that. I…um…think I need to get some fresh air.'

She frowned. 'Where are you going?'

He'd thought flowers. Maybe something bright and happy. Friendly rather than romantic.

'I'm not sure you want me around right now. I wouldn't blame you…'

'And you're getting out while the going's good?'

'Yeah. Something like that.'

She smiled, and Jamie felt relief flood through him. They'd said the words, but her real acceptance of his apology was in her smile.

'I want you in that chair. Right now.' She pointed to the seat on the other side of her desk, where Jamie had set up his laptop to work.

Jamie swallowed hard. That was rather more costly than the price of a few flowers, but then Anna had never shied away from difficult. It was the least he could do. He sat down, expecting her to retreat to the other side of her desk, but she pulled up a chair and sat beside him.

'Jon's not the only one who needs a bit of help, is he?'

'I'm dealing with it.'

'I can see that.' Her lips quirked into a half-smile. 'How do you reckon that's going? On a scale of one to ten…?'

Messing up with Anna had made him realise two things. He couldn't just forget about what Jon had done, and he cared for Anna. Right now the level of pain and confusion he was feeling was off any scale he could think of.

'I haven't made much of a start. Nought out of ten would be pushing it.'

'You're here. You're helping your brother. That's huge, Jamie, and I think that entitles you to at least a five.'

'That's generous of you.'

Anna took a breath, regarding him for a moment. Jamie didn't really want to know what she was thinking, but he didn't get to duck away from anything right now.

'What did you argue about? You and Jon?'

'It was… I guess *in the past* isn't going to wash, is it?' So many of the kids he dealt with talked about things that were in their pasts that still held sway over them now.

'No. I think you know the reasons why not. Whatever this is, it's tearing you up and you need to talk about it. If not to me, then someone else, but I really want to help.'

Jamie took a deep breath. 'When it happened, most of my family insisted on taking sides. Caroline was so furious with Jon that she wouldn't even speak to him. I hated it, and I reckoned that if I never spoke about it then they'd come round eventually. I didn't want our argument to rip the family apart, but it did.'

'Caroline's here now.'

'Yes, but it took me a while to convince her to come. I don't want you to think less of Jon, the way my family did. You're his surgeon, he needs you.'

'We practise medicine without fear or favour, Jamie. You know that. Anyway, I *was* Jon's surgeon. I'm not any more.'

'I just didn't want you to feel a conflict.'

'I don't. I know exactly where I stand. You're the person who matters to me, and if you ask me to make no judgement then I'll do my best to respect that. I might have an opinion, but I won't allow it to change the way I act.'

The sudden warmth in his chest almost made him choke. *He* mattered to Anna. Maybe she'd been giving Jon a little extra attention for his sake, and the thought made his accusations seem even viler.

'It'll stay between you and me?'

She nodded. 'Yes, of course. Between friends and in the strictest confidence.'

Jamie leaned back in his seat. Suddenly this felt like the safe place where he could admit to his feelings, without making the situation worse.

'Thanks. I'd like that.'

CHAPTER SIX

WHATEVER IT WAS, it was bad. But she'd told Jamie that she wouldn't judge and so she should just listen, and take whatever he said at whatever value he chose to give it.

'It was Christmas, nearly three years ago. Jon had landed back in the country the previous week, and he was staying at a hotel five minutes from my parents' place. I went up there the day before Christmas Eve with my fiancée, and Caroline was going to drive over with her husband and children on Christmas Day. The idea was that we'd be close, without giving my mother all the extra work of having house guests for a week.'

Fiancée? Anna resisted the urge to take just that one word from everything else that Jamie had said, and nodded him on.

'It was good to see him again. We'd grown apart since I'd gone to medical school and he'd gone on the road…' Jamie shrugged. 'Gill hadn't met him before, but of course she knew him by reputation. She was really thrilled to meet him.'

'Gill, your…erm…' Anna waved her hand, not wanting to say the word.

'Fiancée, yes. She and Jon got on really well, and I was tired, I'd been working pretty hard in the run-up to Christmas. I went to bed and left them talking. I woke up the next morning and she wasn't there.'

'Wasn't…where?' Anna felt her throat dry suddenly.

'Wasn't next to me in bed. She'd been in Jon's room all night.'

'Talking?' Anna decided not to jump to the obvious and most devastating conclusion.

'No. My twin brother slept with my fiancée, after only knowing her for a matter of about six hours. On the night before Christmas Eve. While I was sleeping a couple of rooms along the corridor.'

'He… She…' Anna clapped her hand over her mouth before she said something stupid, feeling her eyes fill with tears. 'Oh, Jamie…'

'Yeah.' He was clearly fighting for control

over his emotions. 'Don't say it. Whatever it is, it's not going to help.'

'No. I don't imagine it will.'

'I looked for her, and then knocked on Jon's door to see if he knew where she'd got to. I was worried about her…' Jamie shook his head. 'She was there, with him. Both dressed in those towelling robes that the hotel provides for guests.'

'And…they'd definitely…' This line of questioning wasn't working very well. She couldn't imagine any sane woman choosing Jon over Jamie, and she couldn't put it into words.

'Like a fool, I just took it for granted that it was all innocent and for some reason Gill had decided to use Jon's shower instead of ours. She followed me back to my room and told me. She was sorry, but Jon had swept her off her feet. She'd found something special and she had to follow her heart.'

'I can't…' She *had* to pull herself together. 'I mean, I believe what you're saying to me. I just can't believe it happened.'

'Neither could I. I didn't trust myself to say anything, I just walked away. I must have walked for miles, and then I decided that I had to talk to them both and went back to the hotel. They'd both packed their things. Jon had the decency to look pretty shamefaced about it all, and I was pretty angry.'

'I think you had a right to be.'

'It didn't help much, though. I tried to keep my cool, but I couldn't. I ended up shouting, asking Gill why she couldn't have just stopped and thought about it before she decided that sleeping with my brother was a good idea, and she burst into tears and turned to *him.* I decided there was nothing more that I could say, and I wasn't going to trade insults, so I turned and walked out. I went to my room and stayed there until after they'd left.'

'Where is she now?' Anna wondered whether Gill was still with Jon but had stayed away from the clinic because of Jamie.

'I don't know. She and Jon broke up after a couple of months, and I heard she was back in England, but she never contacted me. I didn't want to contact her, to be honest. The thing that hurt the most…' Suddenly Jamie's composure cracked and he shook his head.

Anna reached forward, taking his hands in hers. He'd already shown a lot of restraint in telling his story, and maybe that was the real problem. Now that he'd finally accessed his emotions, he needed to own them.

'What was the worst thing, Jamie?'

He looked up at her, his eyes brimming with tears. Anna held onto his hands tightly.

'Stick with me. The worst thing, what was it?'

He pulled one of his hands away from hers, brushing it across his face. But the other hand was still hanging tightly onto hers.

'The worst thing, was the fact that it didn't last. If it had really been something special, and they'd found true love, then maybe I could have come to terms with it. But they'd broken my heart and thrown me away for…a couple of months.'

'And now you're trying to forgive him.'

'He's my brother. I have to forgive him before the rest of the family will. I *want* to forgive him…'

'Do you know why he did it?'

'We never spoke about it.' Jamie shrugged. 'He did it because he could, I guess.'

'I'm so sorry this happened, Jamie.' There was nothing else that she could say, no way to make sense of it all. Maybe just being here was enough.

It seemed enough, for this moment at least. They sat in silence, holding hands. It felt as if there was a measure of healing there, but there had to be more than this if Jamie was ever going to truly leave this behind.

'Could I suggest something?'

He smiled. 'Go ahead. I'm out of ideas in finding a way forward.'

'You haven't talked much about this, have you?'

There was a flash of understanding in Jamie's eyes. 'There are counsellors attached to my charity. I never really got around to talking to any of them…'

'They might not be the best people to talk to, you know them and have a relationship with them outside the counselling sessions. Jon's benefitted from the sessions he's had here, at the clinic.'

'You think I should take part in his sessions?' Jamie shook his head. 'I'm pretty sure that neither of us are quite ready for that.'

'I don't imagine you are. But maybe if you talk to someone here, who's working within the same framework as his counsellor, that might turn into a reconciliation network for you both. When you and Jon are ready.'

Jamie thought for a moment. 'It…makes sense. It might work. Nothing ventured, I suppose…'

'And you both have a lot to gain. Even if you can't truly forgive him, at least you might know a bit more about what happened and how you feel about it. And you'll have tried.' Anna smiled at him. 'Made the best of what you have.'

'Now you're throwing my own words at me.' Jamie's charity was all about teenagers making the best of themselves. 'Don't you have any scruples at all?'

Anna chuckled. 'No. Not many.'

None at all when it came to Jamie. Right now, she'd do anything to help him feel better about this.

'It's a good idea and I'll think about it. Very seriously.' He gave her hand a squeeze and Anna squeezed back. 'Where are you, in all of this?'

That was a question that bore thinking about.

'Practically speaking… Our tissue viability nurse can deal with Jon's burns, and now that we've delayed surgery I'll be taking a step back. I'd like to speak to Dr Lewis and make it formal that I'm no longer Jon's surgeon.'

Jamie knew what that meant. She still had a duty of care to Jon because he was a patient at the clinic, but she was more free to dictate the nature of her relationship with *him*.

'And…' He was still uncertain. Jamie needed her to say this.

'It means I have no part in Jon's counselling or yours. I'm just your friend.'

His moss-green eyes became suddenly luminescent. Slowly Jamie raised her hand and even though his lips barely touched her fingers the effect was electric.

'There's no *just* about having you as a friend.'

Jamie was sitting in the cafeteria with a young girl of around ten. *Young lady* described her better. Her dark hair was done in a neat plait and she wore a pink sweatshirt with matching pink baseball boots and jeans. A pretty blue backpack hung over the back of her seat, and both she and Jamie were sipping their drinks from cups and saucers. A book with a sparkly pink cover lay on the table between them.

It looked like the kind of conversation that shouldn't be interrupted, and Anna decided to collect her coffee and drink it in her office. But Jamie saw her and raised his hand, beckoning her over.

'Anna, this is Jessica. Will you join us?'

Jamie's invitation was obviously sincere, and Jessica turned and smiled too. Anna pulled up a chair and sat down.

'Hi, Jessica. I'm Anna.'

'Anna's my friend,' Jamie explained to Jessica, who nodded, taking the information at face value even if it prompted a small quiver in Anna's heart. 'Jess is Caroline's eldest.'

'We're having tea.' The tone of Jess's voice indicated that this was an established ritual between Jamie and his niece. 'It's nice to have an adult conversation sometimes.'

Jamie chuckled. 'Yeah, it is, isn't it? Jess has younger brothers and between them things can get a little loud.'

'Do you have brothers?' Jess turned to Anna.

'No, I'm an only child.' Since this was an adult conversation, a little honesty was in order. 'I had loads of adult conversation when I was your age. I often wished I had brothers or sisters.'

Jess considered the thought. 'I like my brothers. Most of the time.'

'How many do you have?' Anna had seen Caroline with the baby and an older boy, and Caroline had joked that she was bringing the children to see their Uncle Jon in instalments so they could each get to know him on their own terms.

'Three.'

'The twins are five. And then there's Joshua, he's going to be a year old next month.' Jamie elaborated.

'That sounds like a lot of noise.'

Jess nodded. 'Yes, it is sometimes. They're not allowed in my room. Mum says that's just for me.'

Anna imagined that Jess's room would be neat and tidy, probably with a bit of pink and a lot of sparkle. Her special place. And she had her Uncle Jamie to take her for tea and some adult conversation. It was nice of him to think of doing that.

Jess had finished her drink and was sliding

her book carefully into her backpack. Jamie grinned. 'You're going back upstairs to see your mum and Uncle Jon?'

'Yes. Don't forget what I told you, Uncle Jamie.'

Jamie spread his hand across his heart, in the expression of innocence that always made Anna smile. 'No, of course not. You remember the way…?'

Jess rolled her eyes. 'You don't need to come with me, Uncle Jamie. I can go on my own.'

'Yes, of course you can. I'll just walk you to the door, then, I'm going to get some more tea.' He flashed the hint of a wink at Anna.

She watched as Jamie lingered by the entrance to the cafeteria, obviously watching Jess along the corridor and towards the stairs that led straight up to Jon's ward. He turned, pulling his phone from his pocket and speaking a few words into it, before going to the counter and ordering a cup of coffee. Presumably Caroline now knew to expect her daughter's arrival at any moment.

'That's very sweet of you…' Anna smiled at him as he sat back down.

'You think so?' That innocent look again.

'I'm always up for a bit of adult conversation too. Jess has decided she wants to take me in hand.'

He pushed his half-drunk cup of herbal tea to one side and took a sip of the coffee. Clearly he and Jess had their own set of rules for tea drinking, which stipulated they should both have the same herbal blend, but Jamie preferred coffee.

'She knows about you and Jon?'

Jamie shrugged. 'She was old enough when the argument happened to know that something really bad was going on. Not old enough to understand it properly. That's not easy for her.'

Anna's own childhood had been full of carefully explained things, all of them age appropriate. She'd never had brothers and sisters, or uncles and aunts, whose actions were a mystery to her.

'But you've explained things to her.'

'She knows that her twin brothers argue, and then make up and turn into the best of friends again. I told her that when you're grown up things sometimes get a bit more complicated, but that I'll always love her and so will her

Uncle Jon.' Jamie quirked his lips down. 'Caroline will make sure that Jon keeps to his end of that bargain.'

'Not you?'

Jamie laughed suddenly. 'You and Jess would get on like a house on fire. She's made me a list of five things I have to do.'

'She has? Good girl! I hope you've taken note.'

'I did. I take note of everything you say as well.' The humour in his eyes couldn't conceal their warmth. 'I told her that taking him shopping to get him a present wasn't really our style, so we agreed on going to the pub for a quiet drink together. Although we'll have to choose our spot if we don't want to be besieged by Jon's fans.'

Jamie's easy relationship with his niece was nice, he was the protective adult who kept his niece from harm, but they could still talk as equals. Anna had been fascinated by the complex interactions of a large family when she'd been married, and she missed them. Now the only place she could find them was here, at the clinic, and she felt pretty much the same as Jess obviously did. If she could make peace, she would.

'Your…um…name came up. In my counselling session.' Jamie was staring into his coffee now.

'Yes? That's okay, you don't have to explain. It's between you and your counsellor.' Anna could feel her ears starting to burn all the same.

'There's nothing that says I can't mention it either.' Jamie shot her a thoughtful smile.

'No. There isn't.' Anna was holding her breath. This was stupid, Jamie's counselling sessions were none of her business. She still wanted to know what he'd said about her. Or maybe she didn't…

'I was talking about the weekend. You know I'm taking Jon down to my place in Hastings on Saturday, and Caroline's bringing the children over?'

'Yes, Caroline mentioned it the other day. Seems like a good idea. Jon's been much better these last few days and it'll do him good…' The words dried in Anna's throat. This wasn't about Jon. It was about Jamie.

'I was saying that you'd supported us both

in keeping the lid on things. I wasn't sure how we'd do on our own. Caroline's great but she's too close to it all and she gets upset when there's any hint of an argument between Jon and me.'

'He's been baiting you, hasn't he?' Anna had noticed the jibes that Jon aimed at his brother from time to time. Jamie was one of the most easygoing people she knew, and he ignored them, but Anna could see him making an effort to hold his anger back.

'Jon's always been the more impatient of the two of us. He's making a good show of things, and claiming he's better and stronger now, but he's still fragile. My role is to keep the peace and help him as much as I can.'

It was an approach. One that clearly took more heed of Jon's needs than Jamie's. 'You might be right. What do you want of me, Jamie?'

'It's a big ask…' He quirked his lips down. 'Not much notice either, you're probably busy…'

'All right, so you've supplied me with an excuse to say no. You'd better give me a chance to use it.'

Jamie chuckled. 'I was wondering if you fancied joining us. Not as an arbiter between me and Jon, just for a day out and some lunch together. Although I might glance in your direction from time to time, just to remind myself that I *do* need to keep a lid on things.'

Jamie needed this. Badly. He wouldn't have asked if he hadn't.

'This is your family day, Jamie. Won't Caroline feel I'm intruding?'

'I mentioned it to her and she thought it was a great idea, if you'd like to come. She was expecting that her husband Harry would be there, but he has a meeting with a client who's only in the country for a couple of days so it had to be Saturday. Harry runs his own architectural practice and this client wants to talk about a new project, so Caroline told him he must go and that she'd be all right on her own. I think she's rather hoping she won't end up being the only adult in the room.'

'And what are you hoping?' Jamie had tried so hard to keep his feelings under control and Anna had seen the toll it had taken on him.

'I'm *planning* on being the perfect host. Caroline knows that, but she thinks your presence might remind both Jon and me that we still need to make an effort. She reckons that you have us both twisted around your little finger at the moment.' He shot her his most compelling innocent look, and Anna's heart jumped in her chest. 'I haven't a clue what she means, and I told her that she was imagining things.'

Twisted around her little finger. It was a breath-taking thought, not so much where Jon was concerned but Jamie... And he wanted her to be a part of his family day. Anna felt herself flush.

'I've embarrassed you. It's a bad idea, I shouldn't have asked...' Jamie's face registered concern, and he was back-pedalling furiously now.

It would take just one nod to take everything off the table. They could finish their coffee, and Anna could go on to put the finishing touches to her non-existent plans for Saturday. That might be the best way forward, but Jamie needed her. If she needed reminding that he was just a friend, then she could imagine the look he gave her when he said it. As if friends were the most important thing in the world.

'You *should* have asked. Because I'd like to come.'

'Really?' He seemed genuinely surprised.

'We could have an adult conversation, if you like. About the weather, or something inconsequential.'

Jamie laughed. 'That would be fantastic.'

CHAPTER SEVEN

SATURDAY MORNING WAS gloomy and overcast, but when Jon walked out of the clinic, with his brother by his side, he greeted the drizzle of rain and the open air with a broad smile.

Anna had hung back, wondering if Jon would take the front seat, but he held the door open for her and then climbed into the back of the car. Jamie didn't even seem to notice his brother's show of gallantry, and Anna settled into her seat. As they drove out of London the skies seemed to clear a little, and by the time they reached Sussex, the sun was out.

The old farmhouse stood back from the road a little. A silver SUV was parked in the drive outside, indicating that Caroline was already here with the children, and when they approached the door it flew open.

'Uncle Jamie…' The twins ran towards Jamie, and he bent to pick them both up, one under each arm, and whirl them around.

'What have you two terrors been doing?'

'Making gingerbread men. Mum said it was all right for us to cook.'

Jamie chuckled. 'Oh, she did, did she? I'll be having a word with your mother if she's left a mess. Did you make one for Uncle Jon?'

'Yes!'

Jon had been watching, still a little reserved around the children. He broke into a sudden smile, and Jamie put the twins back down onto their feet. 'Why don't you show him, then?'

Ben, the more reserved of the two, hung back, but Thomas took Jon's hand, pulling him into the house. Jamie smirked, pleased with the welcome, and Anna followed him inside. Coats were taken off and piled onto the hall-stand, and Jon was propelled through the hall-way and into the kitchen.

There *was* a mess, along with the smell of cooking, but Jamie didn't heed it. Caroline was doing her best to get icing out of her baby son's hair, while Jess had a stack of fine china plates in front of her, none of which matched, and was clearly deciding which plate went best with which gingerbread man.

'That one's yours, Uncle Jon.' Thomas waved

his finger towards a figure with a large yellow splodge of icing around its chest. 'We made a guitar.'

'That's great.' Jon was all smiles now.

'Did you make one for Anna?' Jamie asked Ben, and he nodded.

'Of course we did. You're the one with the yellow icing all over your head, Anna.' Caroline grinned at her. 'A bit like Joshua. The twins reckoned it was a good idea to ice him as well.'

'Go and sit down, I'll make the coffee while Jess finishes putting out the plates.' Jamie smiled at his niece, who grinned back at him.

'No, I need to clear up a bit...' Caroline protested, but Jamie was shooing everyone out of the kitchen.

'I'll do that. It's easier when no one's making icing-sugar footprints all over the place.'

'Oh! The carpets... Thomas and Ben, take your shoes off,' Caroline wailed, and Anna bent down, helping the twins with their shoelaces.

Order was restored, and Jon lowered himself into an armchair, seeming tired after the journey. The children were left to play by the fireplace, and Anna had a moment to look around.

Jamie's sitting room was…different. The room had obviously been stripped back at some point, but no effort had been made to cover the cracks in the brickwork over the fireplace, they'd just been filled. The old polished floorboards were pitted and stained from years of wear, and the deep brick fireplace had obviously seen many years of use. But above it the long wooden mantel was pristine and gleaming, with glass lamps at either end. The sofas and chairs were all spotless, and the book cabinets and furniture gleamed. It was a suffusion of old and new, comfortable but with a lot of character.

'Nice, isn't it?' Caroline had seen her looking around.

'It's lovely. If I'd known that *not* decorating could be so effective, I wouldn't have gone to all the bother at my place. Although I imagine that quite a bit of thought went into this.'

'Yes, it did. When Jamie bought this place, it was pretty run down. He decided that anything you touched would be new and clean. Anything you didn't touch would be left as it was. I was a bit sceptical, but my husband Harry's an architect and he got it. I do now too, I think it works.'

As long as you had the eye to pick out furniture that didn't match but which went together well. Chairs and sofas that were all different but were upholstered in complementary colours, dark reds and russet tones. It seemed artless, but there was a cohesiveness of thought behind it all.

Jessica appeared, carefully holding two plates, each with a gingerbread man on it. She gave one to Jon and one to Anna, and Anna thanked her for choosing the prettiest plate for her. Jess confided that it was her favourite too, then disappeared back into the kitchen for the next two. Jamie brought the coffee, and the twins were persuaded to sit down in a couple of wooden children's chairs that stood by the fireplace.

'So…why have I got green hair?' Jamie was regarding his plate with a smile.

'The green icing was meant to be for your eyes.' Caroline shrugged. 'Call it artistic licence.'

'Yes. Of course.' Jamie bit the leg off his gingerbread man. 'They taste great, Jessica.'

Jessica gave him a little smile, obviously pleased that her part in it all hadn't gone unnoticed by her uncle.

'You've done a lot here since I saw it last.' Jon was looking around the sitting room. 'It looks great.'

'You want to see the rest?' Jamie asked diffidently.

'Yes, thanks. That would be great.'

There was a restrained courtesy about Jamie and Jon's conversations, but they were talking and it obviously meant a lot to Jon to be asked here. A shared glance between her and Jamie was enough for Anna to tag along with them, curious to see what he'd done in the rest of the house.

Jamie's eclectic style was everywhere. In the dining room, a large polished table was surrounded by cabinets filled with books and a collection of plates, glasses and silverware, some matching and some not. Jamie walked straight past a corridor that led to the other side of the one-storey house, and Anna guessed that the bedrooms lay in that direction. Jon ignored it as well, which was probably just as well.

Only the kitchen and bathroom showed no trace of the building's ancient shell, with gleaming floor-to-ceiling tiles and mirrors in the bathroom, and wooden cabinets in the kitchen. When Jamie led the way out of the kitchen door, Anna found herself on a long veranda.

'This must be lovely in the summer.' The view was spectacular, farmland and open countryside stretching off into the distance.

Jamie nodded. 'I like it in winter, too. I've a couple of space heaters, and it's quite cosy out here. Last year I sat and watched it snow.'

The thought of him sitting alone seemed a little sad. But the house was full of noise and activity now, some of which was heading their way. The twins burst out onto the veranda, and Thomas ran up to Jamie, pulling at his hand.

'Why don't you show Uncle Jon our cars…'

Jamie grinned, squatting down in front of the two boys. 'What cars?'

'The ones we're building, silly… Uncle Jon would like to see them.' Thomas turned to Jon for confirmation.

Jon was clearly torn, unable to say no to his nephew but clearly wanting to show how much he appreciated Jamie's hospitality as well. 'I'd like to see them later, Thomas. Uncle Jamie's showing me around right now.'

The twins chorused their disappointment and Jamie smiled.

'Okay, why don't you two show Uncle Jon your model cars now, then? He might have some ideas about what colours to paint them.' Jamie glanced up at Jon. 'The garden will still be here later.'

'Okay. Thanks.' Jon grinned, holding his hands out to the twins and they started to pull him back into the house.

It was a nice gesture. The two boys were still a little shy with Jon, and Jamie seemed determined to include his brother as much as he could. He knew how much that meant to Jon.

He watched Jon go, and then turned to Anna. 'Looks as if we have ten minutes for one of those adult conversations you promised me. Would you like to see what I've done in the garden?'

'Yes. That sounds great.' Anna glanced down at her high-heeled boots. 'I've got a pair of trainers in my bag. Caroline said that I might need them if we all decided to go for a walk.'

Jamie nodded. 'Yeah, good idea. I'll wait for you here…'

The garden was much the same as the house. Seemingly artless, but everywhere there were things that made you want to stop and look. An old, worn stone birdbath nestled amongst the foliage. Blackberry bushes, forming a wide mass of ripening fruit that could be picked and eaten straight away, and the soft yellows of a brick-built outhouse contrasted with the new, dark slate roof. It was shaped by nature, but Jamie's guiding hand had given it a touch of magic.

'How long have you been here?' They strolled together along a winding pathway that led away from the house.

'Six years.' Jamie looked around at the garden. 'It's not really finished yet.'

'It looks like one of those things that will never quite be finished.' There were no straight lines about this place, it seemed as if it might constantly evolve.

'No, I'm not sure it will.'

'I expected something different. A bit more under control.' Anna smiled up at him and he gave her a *Who? Me?* smile.

'You think I'm a control freak?'

'You have goals, don't you?'

Jamie chuckled. 'That's a different thing. I have goals, I just don't make myself any promises about how I'm going to find my way to them.'

That made sense. The way that everything fitted together neatly, without necessarily matching. 'Caroline said the place was pretty run down when you bought it. It must have taken a lot of work.'

'It's the closest thing I have to a hobby. I work hard, and then when I come down here I relax and go with the flow of the place.' Jamie turned, his hands in his pockets, looking back at the house.

'I had an inkling of its potential when I bought it, but after I'd had the rubbish and old furniture from the last owner carted away, it started to take shape. The plaster was damaged and rotten, but once that was stripped out and the carpets were lifted there was this amazing space. It seemed somehow wrong to cover it all up.'

'Is that what they call *arrested decay*?'

Jamie shrugged. 'Not entirely. I removed the worst of the decay, rather than arresting it. I wouldn't like to say what you'd call this.'

So he wasn't even going to give it a name. Anna could see how that was Jamie's version of therapy, a break from the exacting work that he did. Or maybe in its own way it was another version of his work. Knowing where he wanted to be, and letting the journey define itself.

'Isn't it a bit lonely here sometimes?' Anna bit her tongue. It *was* a large house for just one person, but then Jamie had probably never intended to be alone here.

'Being on my own wasn't in the plan.'

'Sorry. I didn't mean to…you know.'

'That's okay. It happened. Things aren't what I expected but I'm lucky in lots of ways. Whenever I feel the urge to fill the house with kids, I just give Caroline a call. She's generally got a few I can borrow.'

So he'd wanted children. Of course he had. He was so good with his nephews and niece and they obviously thought the world of their Uncle Jamie. It was a sobering reminder that getting too close to him would only lead to heartbreak.

'You never wanted to settle down?'

'I'm settled. I have a flat and a career.' Anna deliberately avoided the obvious intent of his question.

'Yeah.' He started to walk slowly away from the house again.

Perhaps she'd been a bit short with him. There was no reason why she shouldn't give him the basic facts.

'I was married six years ago, but it didn't take. We split up after a year.'

'I'm sorry to hear that.'

'It's okay. We never really should have been together. We wanted different things.' Anna and Daniel had actually wanted exactly the same things. They'd both wanted children, and even though he'd promised that he would be happy with their family of two, he'd changed his mind.

'It changes your view of things, though, doesn't it? You think you're going in one direction and suddenly you find you're not.' Jamie was looking at her thoughtfully.

'Yes, it does. But that's in the past now. I love my job, and most of my energy goes into that.'

He didn't answer. Maybe he didn't believe her, the married-to-my-job thing hadn't sounded totally convincing. But Anna had said all she was going to say, and thankfully he left it alone.

'Would you like to see the beehives?' They were wandering further and further from the house.

'You have beehives? How much land do you have here?'

Jamie pointed to a line of trees in the distance. 'It goes down to there. We planted an orchard, and this year I'll have some apples. There are bees and a wildflower meadow, and...you see down in that dip?'

Anna followed the direction of his pointing finger. 'Marshlands?'

'It's more a small dip that collects water at the moment. But I'm hoping it'll grow and encourage some wildlife.'

'How do you do all this?' Even Jamie's voracious appetite for work wasn't equal to what had been done here.

'I have help. A couple of the lads from the youth club that the charity runs couldn't get jobs when they left school. They decided to do something for themselves and started a gardening business. I advised them on some of the practicalities and got them onto a course, and then became their first customer.'

'They've done well.' Anna might have guessed that Jamie's nurturing of the land would also extend to nurturing the talents of his young charges.

Jamie chuckled. 'They made up in enthusiasm for what they lacked in experience at first, and we had our share of disasters. But they got things together, and they've got a nice little business going now. They spend a day a week here, and pretend not to mind when I interfere, so it works pretty well.'

'I'd like to see the orchard.'

'No appetite for bees?' He grinned at her.

'They get a bit bad-tempered in the autumn, don't they? I'm not sure I want to be stung.'

Jamie chuckled, turning onto a path that led

to the left. '*My* bees are very good mannered. But since you prefer apples, the orchard's this way.'

He led her towards a collection of young trees, planted far enough apart to allow for more growth. Jamie pointed out the different varieties, some for cooking and some for eating.

'That one looks about ready.' He pointed up at a red apple in the branches above Anna's head. 'Want to try it?'

'I'd love to, thanks…' Anna reached up, and even when she stood on her toes her fingertips didn't quite make contact. 'Can you reach it?'

'They taste better when you've picked them yourself, straight from the tree.' Jamie hesitated and then held out his hand. 'You want a boost?'

The apple was hanging right above her head, just begging to be picked. 'Um…yes, okay.'

She felt his hands around her waist and he lifted her against him. Anna curled her arms protectively over her chest, feeling her own body stiffen. The thick layers of clothing between them didn't seem to be doing anything to mitigate the effect of being so close to Jamie.

'Um... It would help if you hung on...' Anna could hear the strain in his voice. She was dead weight in his arms, and Jamie was clearly struggling a bit to support her.

'Sorry...' Winding her legs around his waist was easier than she'd thought. More natural. And when she clung to his shoulder with one hand, it seemed almost the proper thing to do.

'That's better.' He balanced himself and Anna suddenly felt safe and strong. She reached for the apple, turning it in her hand.

'Oh. This one has a hole in it.'

'Pick it anyway, it can be used for cooking. What about that one...?'

The apple that hung a little higher was ruby red and perfect. When she bent it upwards, the stalk separated from the branch easily, a sure sign that it was ready to harvest.

'Got it.'

He let her down carefully. When her feet hit the ground again it was almost a disappointment to have to step away from him. Anna inspected the apple carefully for any holes or damage.

'Now close your eyes.' Jamie's lips curved. It was the kind of smile that no woman in her right mind would want to miss a moment of, but Anna closed her eyes, sinking her teeth into the apple.

It tasted fresh and sweet. So much more like a real apple than the ones she bought in the supermarket.

'This is gorgeous. You want a taste…?' She opened her eyes.

He nodded, his eyes darkening suddenly. Moss green, and glistening with a desire that provoked an immediate response in Anna's chest. Suddenly she forgot all about the apple.

When she stepped towards him, his hand touched the waist of her jacket. So softly that she didn't even feel it. She wanted very badly to feel everything about his embrace, and everything that told her she shouldn't was shattered beneath the weight of expectation of his touch.

She had to move. Either forward or back. Forward was the only way that seemed clear at the moment. Anna reached up, allowing her fingertips to brush his cheek.

It was a sweet, slow give and take. Staring

into each other's eyes, watching for the response to each new action. The increasing pressure of his hand on her waist. Anna laid her hand on his shoulder and they were almost in an embrace. One that she wanted so very much. She stood on her toes, kissing his cheek lightly, and felt him pull her a little closer.

This was delicious, but it could end at any moment. He could decide that he'd misinterpreted all the signs, or that he needed something more definite and draw back.

'I want to kiss you.'

Jamie smiled. 'I'd love to kiss you back.'

That was that, then. Still he didn't move, waiting for her to take things at whatever pace she wanted. Head-spinningly fast seemed like a wonderful option. Anna stood on her toes, kissing his lips.

She tasted apple-sweet and dew-fresh. When he drew her a little closer, Jamie felt her arms tighten around his neck, pulling him down. In a moment of sheer exhilaration he realised that she wanted this just as much as he did.

He couldn't conceal his hunger. When he kissed her again, she responded and Jamie felt his whole body harden. She was so soft and yet so strong.

'Did I forget to tell you how beautiful—?'

She stopped his words with another kiss.

'Yes, you forgot. You mentioned that my hair was coming loose from my ponytail the other day.'

'Ignore me. I'm a complete and utter jerk.' One who noticed everything about Anna. One who'd been dreaming of this moment for far too long, and telling himself it mustn't happen.

'You're forgiven. After all, this isn't really in your plan, is it?'

A sudden dose of honesty that jerked him back to his senses. 'No, it's not.'

'That's okay. We both have a little baggage.'

So there *was* more to it than she'd said. Jamie had suspected that was the case—no one got married and divorced within a year without a few scars to show for it.

'Both of us?'

'There's no story to tell, if that's what you mean.'

'Everyone's got a story. But if you don't want to talk about it, that's fine.'

'Okay. I don't want to talk about it.' She

looked up at him, and Jamie suddenly forgot everything other than the pale blue of her eyes. 'But since we both seem to have settled on the same eventual outcome, then I guess a diversion doesn't matter.'

'*You* are never a diversion.' *That* mattered. That Anna knew how important she was to him, and that this had meant something.

She smiled up at him. 'Thank you. In that case, you can kiss me again.'

He didn't need to be told a second time. If this was the only thing that he could share with Anna, then he wanted it to matter. Jamie kissed her, feeling her move against him, her arms tightening again around his neck.

He'd found another side of Anna. She was passionate and giving and yet she knew how to end things. She made him feel that this hadn't been one big mistake, a lapse of self-control that should be forgotten as soon as possible. No apologies and no regrets. Just an understanding that they should stop before it led somewhere that neither of them was ready to go.

Jamie's head was fine with that. His heart would follow if he repeated the words enough times, but right now it didn't know how to beat without taking up her rhythm. Without thrilling at her smile as they collected cooking apples that had fallen from the low cordons at one end of the orchard, filling their pockets with them.

'Apple and blackberry?' They'd started on their way back to the house, and Anna stopped by the bushes. Jamie nodded, cupping his hands to receive the blackberries as she picked them.

'We'll give them to Caroline. She can use them for a pie tomorrow.'

Anna nodded, popping a blackberry into her mouth. 'Mmm… They're sweet. Try one.'

She laughed as he shrugged, his hands too full to comply. Anna made a show of searching amongst the branches, curved and heavy with fruit, until she found a large blackberry.

'This one looks nice.' She popped it into his mouth, and Jamie smiled.

'Yeah. That's the best one.'

'Hold on a minute…' She raised her juice-stained fingers to his mouth, and he felt her wipe away a smudge. 'That's better.'

He could do this for the rest of the morning,

and the better part of the afternoon as well. Then he could sit by the fire with Anna, maybe roasting a few chestnuts as the evening closed in around them. But he had guests and it was about time he made a start on lunch, even if it was just a matter of putting the lasagne he'd made into the oven and taking the salad out of the fridge.

'We'd better go back. You have important work to do today.' Anna was smiling up at him.

'Yeah. Though to be honest, I'd rather be here…'

'I know. But this is an opportunity that you can't miss.'

His family, together again. It was something that Jamie wanted, even though it was hard. Out here he could forget about the anger that was never too far from the surface every time he saw Jon. Anna seemed to know, and she turned without another word, leading the way back to the house.

CHAPTER EIGHT

THE DAY WAS going well. They'd had lunch, and then Jessica and the twins had gone out into the garden. Jamie had lit the fire in the sitting room, leaving Jon to doze in front of it, and when Caroline had chased him out of the kitchen, he'd meandered out into the garden to see what the children were up to.

'He's great with the kids.' Caroline had reached the end of a long succession of plates and pans, and picked up a teacloth to help Anna with the drying up. 'It's a shame…'

'That he doesn't have any of his own?' Anna tried to clear the lump that was forming in her throat.

'Yes. I can't blame him for being cautious, not after what happened with Gill. He'd be happier if he could leave that behind, though.'

'Maybe he can. He and Jon seem to be patching things up.'

'You think so?' Caroline didn't look convinced.

'I don't really know. They seem…'

'Polite. They're mostly polite with each other. Apart from when Jon's baiting Jamie, and Jamie's trying not to notice.'

Anna sighed. 'Yes. But it's a start.'

Joshua was starting to fret a little in his baby bouncer, and Caroline picked him up. Anna made a face at him, and he chuckled.

'Will you hold him while I put everything away?' Joshua was reaching for Anna, and Caroline put him into her arms. She sat down at the kitchen table, and the little boy started to grab at her hair.

'He has green eyes!' The resemblance to Jamie took her breath away.

Caroline laughed. 'Yes, it's not fair, is it? I got stuck with muddy brown in the genetic lottery, and now my son has gorgeous green eyes. I thought they might get darker as he gets older, but my mum said that Jamie and Jon's were exactly the same, so I'm keeping my fingers crossed.'

Anna hugged the little boy and he gurgled happily, clutching at her sweater. This was as close as she'd ever get to knowing what it would be like to hold Jamie's child, and even though it hurt she couldn't let him go. She felt a tear roll down her cheek, and brushed it away before Caroline could see it.

'He's so precious…' She heard her voice falter as she said the words.

'You're reckoning on having some of your own?' Caroline lifted a pile of plates into one of the cupboards and then grinned over her shoulder.

If only. If she could give Jamie a green-eyed, happy little boy like this, Anna would have let things between them go much further. She'd have hung in there and shown him that the heartbreak they'd both suffered was in the past and could be turned around. But that was all wishful thinking.

'I don't know. I'm pretty busy with my career.' Anna shrugged trying to shift the pain in her chest.

'The two aren't necessarily mutually exclusive. I've put things on hold a bit workwise, but I still work two days a week. It keeps me relatively sane.'

'What do you do?' Changing the subject

from babies to Caroline's job would be good right now.

'I'm a midwife. Harry and I decided that Joshua would be our last. I wouldn't mind more, but there's the small matter of raising them to contend with. We have our hands full as it is—people say that twins are more than twice the work, and it's true...'

Caroline was talking still, but the words seemed to fade into background noise. Anna had come to terms with her inability to have children, and after Daniel had left her she'd pulled herself together and got her life back on track. She should forget all about things that she couldn't do and concentrate on the ones she could. But the child in her lap was making that very difficult.

Caroline walked over to the window, looking outside. 'The kids are amusing themselves out there so let's have some coffee, eh?'

'Oh. Yes, that would be nice.' Perhaps she could give Joshua back to his mother and the terrible, instinctive tug would begin to subside.

'Where's Jamie, I wonder? He might want...'

Caroline fell silent as voices from the sitting

room floated through into the kitchen. They were getting louder.

'You just walked away, Jamie!'

'Oh. Right. And that made it all okay, did it? Sleeping with my fiancée was obviously the only response possible to my career choices.'

'Oh, no! Just when I thought things were going so well…' Caroline wailed, her hand flying to her mouth.

This didn't sound good. The two women ignored Joshua's innocent babble, straining to hear.

'I needed you. We had a dream, and you turned your back on it.'

'You had a dream, Jon. It was all about you. It always is.'

A thud sounded from the sitting room as if something had been thrown. Caroline jumped, tears beginning to roll down her cheeks. She must have been dreading this.

Anna stood, putting Joshua into his mother's arms. 'I'm going to stop this.'

'How?'

'I've no idea…' All she knew was that she had to. For Jamie's sake. She marched into the sitting room and saw the two of them on their feet, each trying to stare the other down. The book that had been sitting on the coffee table, next to Jon's chair, was lying upended in the grate.

'Stop it!'

Jamie flinched at the sound of her voice, taking a step back, but Jon flailed his arms towards his brother.

'That's right. Play the injured party, why don't you…'

'I said stop it.' Anna pushed between them, feeling Jamie's hand on her shoulder, gently trying to move her out of the way. She shook it off, facing Jon. 'Sit *down*, Jon.'

'Why me?' Jon growled at her and she felt Jamie trying to move her away again.

'Both of you. Back off and sit down.'

For a moment there was silence. Then Jon turned and sat down. Jamie backed away too, sitting down in a chair on the other side of the fireplace. Anna took a deep breath.

'You should both be ashamed of yourselves. If you want to shout then you can do it out of earshot of Caroline and the children. Don't you think they've suffered enough?'

Jamie's face, set in an expression of anger

and stress, softened a little. 'I'm sorry. I'll go and see if they're okay—'

'You aren't going anywhere, Jamie. I'm not finished with either of you yet. What's all this about?'

'He—' Anna silenced Jon with a wave of her hand.

'No, Jon. You both need to stop blaming each other and start taking responsibility for your own actions.'

Jon stared at her, clearly not comprehending her meaning. But Jamie knew, she could see it in his face. If he could just lead the way, maybe Jon would follow. Maybe they could turn this into progress.

Rage. Jon had been baiting him, and he'd lost control of his temper. And then shock when Anna had pushed herself in between him and Jon. Now Jamie felt ashamed of himself for destroying the fragile peace that had been carefully brokered between him and his brother.

But Anna wasn't going to take shame. She wouldn't take apologies or excuses, or promises to keep his cool in the future. She wanted more than that, and there was no denying her.

It occurred to Jamie that she was very beautiful when angry, but he dismissed the thought. Anna didn't want to hear that either. She was standing, her arms folded, waiting for someone to say something, and he knew exactly what he had to do.

'When we were kids…you remember, Jon, how you used to help me with my written work?'

'I remember.' Jon glared at him sullenly.

'I never thought I'd be able to cope with medical school. But you gave me the confidence, you told me that I could do anything.'

'I meant…' Jon puffed out a breath. 'I meant *we* could do anything. We could write songs and perform them. We were going to take the world by storm…'

'All right.' Jon's voice had started to rise, and Anna shot him a warning look. 'Were you good?'

'They were very good.' Tension still hung heavily in the air, and Caroline's voice made Jamie jump. She was standing in the doorway, holding Joshua in her arms.

'You were just a kid.' Jon pursed his lips, but his tone was quieter now, more measured.

'We *were* good together, Jon.' This felt like an admission. Jamie realised that he'd never really voiced it before. He'd been so determined that he wanted to be a doctor that he hadn't allowed himself to even think it.

'So why did you break up the partnership? You could have been famous. It sounds like a nice life to me.' Anna allowed herself a smile.

Jamie shrugged. 'I just felt… I suppose that music was something I did. A doctor is what I am.'

'And you explained that to Jon? After everything he'd done to help you?'

Jamie felt himself redden. 'No, I don't think I did. I'm sorry.'

Anna turned her gaze onto Jon. Jamie felt a prickle of sympathy for his brother because he'd just been subjected to that look and he hadn't been able to resist it.

'Music is what *I* am. I wanted it to be what you were too, but…' Jon shrugged. 'I guess that's life. We don't always get to choose.'

'It sounds as if you resented the way that what each of you wanted led you in different directions.' Anna spoke gently.

Jon let out a grim laugh. 'He wasn't so

much fun. I got the band together and we sang "Everywhere"... It was *his* song, but half the time he was too wrapped up in his books to even notice.'

'I noticed. I was really proud of you. I thought it all went to your head a bit, though.'

'A bit? Trust me, when you're nineteen years old, and you're standing in front of thousands of people all shouting your name, it goes to your head. It loses its charm a bit after a while, though. Everyone seems to want a piece of you.'

Jon had never spoken of this before. Or maybe Jamie had just never listened. 'I should have been there for you more over the years.'

'You had your own gig. Your studies and then that charity of yours... I hear it does a lot of good things.'

There was one more thing that Jamie had to do. He got slowly to his feet, flashing a glance at Anna, and she nodded him on.

'You helped me overcome my dyslexia, and gave me the confidence to chase my dreams, Jon. The charity's just a way of passing that down.' Jamie held his hand out to his brother.

It was no longer a struggle, he really meant it this time.

The handshake turned into a hug. He heard Caroline's squeal of delight, and she rushed over and kissed both of them. When Jamie turned, looking for Anna, she'd flopped back onto the sofa, as if the effort of this had been too much for her. But she was smiling.

'I've brought you both something.' Caroline delivered baby Joshua into Jon's arms and hurried out into the hallway. When she reappeared, she was holding the battered box that contained memories that had seemed lost for ever a moment ago.

'You brought the games!' Jon smiled suddenly.

'It's been a long time since we all played.' Caroline started to unload the board games onto the table. 'I thought we might give it a go. If you'd like to.'

'It sounds like a great idea. I'll make some tea, and fetch the kids in from the garden, shall I?' Jamie volunteered.

There was one thing more that he needed to do before any of that. His gaze found Anna's and she rose, following him into the kitchen.

'Hey. Thank you.' Taking her hand seemed acceptable, and when he did she smiled up at him.

'Are you good with this? Really?'

She'd seen through the pretence and had known that his initial reconciliation with Jon was what Jamie knew he must do, rather than something he felt in his heart. This, more recent, one went a lot deeper.

'I'm good. I mean it this time.' Jamie heaved a sigh. 'All that you said, about taking responsibility for our own actions, telling each other how we felt… I knew that. It's what I tell the families I work with…'

'It's easy to say. Harder to put into practice when you have all the emotion to deal with as well.'

'Are you letting me off lightly? That's not like you.'

She rolled her eyes. 'No. You still don't get any free passes from me. There's a lot of work to do still.'

There was. He and Jon hadn't even got to the point of discussing what had happened at Christmas three years ago. But this was a start. Jamie was beginning to see that it wasn't just an isolated incident but that the resentment had been brewing for years.

Suddenly she stretched out her arms in an invitation that he took straight away. Her hug was comforting and yet sexy all at the same time, and everything he needed right now.

'You can be a bit scary when you want to be.'

He heard her laugh against his chest. 'I can be *very* scary. Don't you forget it.'

'No, ma'am.'

'And I could *really* do with a cup of tea.' Anna looked up at him, mischief in her eyes. 'So you can leave the talking for another time and get on and make me one.'

Caroline's idea of board games was a hit with everyone. The older twins, Jamie and Jon, each paired up with one of the younger ones and faced each other across the board with mock scowls. Jessica added a more ladylike note to the proceedings and sat next to Anna, discussing their next moves in a whisper behind her hand. Baby Joshua sat on his mother's knee, keeping his strategies to himself but holding up his arms, babbling with glee along with everyone else, when someone made a killer move.

A family. One that was weathering a storm but who were all focussed on the same thing. Love had held them together, and maybe it would bring them safely home. For now, Anna was a part of that, but it wouldn't last. She shouldn't get too comfortable here, and she definitely shouldn't think about the green eyes of baby Joshua or his uncle Jamie.

When Caroline packed Jon and all the children into her SUV and drove away, the house seemed suddenly quiet. The plan had been that Jamie would take her to the station so that she could go back to London tonight, but he walked straight past their coats, hanging in the hallway, and stood by the hearth in the sitting room, staring at the glowing coals.

'It feels as if it's been a long day.' Anna was searching for something to say to break the silence.

'Yes, it does.'

'So what are you up to tomorrow?'

He looked up at her, smiling suddenly. 'I have the Hastings Hustlers first thing tomorrow. We're a multi-disciplinary team, but at the moment we're concentrating on basketball.'

'What else do you do?'

'Anything that takes our fancy. We make a mean baseball team, and we play football as well. And tennis. A couple of the girls do gymnastics and we have a chess player too.'

'And they're all Hastings Hustlers?'

'I got the sweatshirts. It seemed a shame to waste them.' Jamie paused for a moment, letting the silence hang between them. 'Would you like to come along? You could meet some of the kids and see something of what we do.'

'I'd love to. Another time perhaps. I'm not sure I can get back down to Hastings for first thing tomorrow morning.'

'You could stay over. You have jeans and trainers and that's all you need to join in. My guest room has plaster on the walls, a proper carpet and all the furniture matches.'

That was a disappointment. Going to sleep in one of the characterful rooms that reflected Jamie's taste would have been nice. But Anna suspected the real piece of information he'd been intending to convey was *guest room.*

'And you get a team sweatshirt. But only if

you play.' He shot her a look that was beyond tempting.

'What colour sweatshirt?' Decorum dictated that she should pretend that the idea wasn't one that demanded an immediate *yes.*

'Red. Only I don't think we have any of those at the moment. Orange, yellow, green, blue, black or violet.'

'No indigo?'

He grinned. Jamie knew that her assent to the plan was only a matter of time. 'Have you tried getting an indigo sweatshirt printed? Black was the closest they could do.'

'Hmm. Violet might be nice. As long as it's not really purple.'

'You can decide for yourself. And I'll stand you lunch afterwards. You can throw some things into the washing machine tonight and they'll be clean for the morning.'

'You know how to tempt a girl, don't you?' This was suddenly so easy. Jamie had staked out the boundaries, and she knew exactly where she stood. A kiss didn't mean that they couldn't just be friends, however explosive it had felt at the time.

'You want temptation? Wait till you see the sweatshirts.'

He led her through the kitchen and into a large office, which caught the best of the early evening sun. It was decorated in the same eclectic style as the sitting room, although a large colour-coded wall planner gave a more businesslike feel. A chrome-legged, fifties-style desk with a shiny red top provided a splash of colour and the sleek computer equipment and shelving contrasted with bare brick walls and a wooden door, knotted and scarred with age. Storage boxes were stacked up against the wall, and Jamie heaved a couple of them to one side, opening them.

'There you go. Pick whichever one you like.'

Anna sorted through the plastic-wrapped sweatshirts. The violet was nice, and she pulled a pile out, sorting through the sizes, which ran from five-to-seven years to extra-large. 'This one will fit.'

'You can't take it out of the bag until you promise to play.' A smile hovered around his lips. Anna tore the plastic, unfolding the sweatshirt and holding it up against herself.

CHAPTER NINE

ANNA WOKE IN a comfortable bed, early morning sunshine filtering through the windows. Unlike her flat in London, the house wasn't overlooked, and she'd left the curtains open, welcoming the glimmer of a harvest moon slanting across the cream-painted walls. Waking at dawn brought the sound of birdsong and not traffic.

The quiet created a sense of peace that the ever-present sounds of the city couldn't reproduce. She'd discovered last night that Jamie didn't own a TV, and they'd sat by the fireside, roasting chestnuts and talking. London was his inspiration, full of the clamour of every different kind of professional and cultural stimulus, but his heart was here.

Her clothes and the new sweatshirt were folded neatly on a chair. Anna gave her T-shirt a shake, deciding that the creases from the washer/dryer would have to fall out with wear, and made for the en suite bathroom.

She found him in the kitchen, wearing a dark green Hastings Hustlers sweatshirt, the white lettering on the back beginning to crack from having been washed and worn.

'Morning. Did you sleep well?'

'Yes, thanks.' Curled up in the bed, wearing borrowed sweatpants and a T-shirt that somehow bore his scent even though they were fresh out of the washing machine. Maybe that had been just in her dreams. There was only one thing that would have been better, and that was on the other side of the boundaries they'd set.

'I've got eggs, bacon, toast… Um, coffee, bananas, peanut butter…'

'Sounds great. Everything but the peanut butter. I'll take the banana for later.'

He gave her a smiling nod. 'I was rather hoping you wouldn't go for a sliver of toast with a dash of low-calorie marmalade. Not that I *have* any low-calorie marmalade.'

'You have regular marmalade, though?'

'I have honey. The bread's from a local bakery and the eggs and bacon are from the farm shop.' He smiled. 'They could probably tell you the name of the hen that laid the egg, but that's a little too personal for my taste. I have absolutely no idea who grew the banana.'

'Sounds delicious.'

An hour later, after a leisurely breakfast that tasted of the countryside instead of the supermarket, they were on the road. Jamie drove into the centre of Hastings, parking the car on the edge of a small park, where a line of basketball courts was currently filled with kids in Hastings Hustlers sweatshirts.

Two older boys were already practising, hotly contesting possession of the ball. There were girls and boys of all ages, and Anna wondered how that was all going to work when it came to picking teams. Jamie seemed satisfied with the turnout, though, and when he got out of the car and they walked over to the basketball courts, everyone crowded around.

'This is Anna, everyone.' A chorus of *hellos* followed and Anna gave a smile and a small wave. 'Shall we pick teams?'

Everyone knew what to do. The two older boys were the team captains and everyone else lined up in order of size. Jamie settled an argument between two girls about who was taller than the other, and then went down the line, dividing everyone up into two teams. He produced a printed chart from his pocket, and started to note down who was playing where.

Callum appeared from the crush, taking off one of his fingerless gloves and displaying the back of his hand. A few black lines still remained and the skin looked a little red, but the letters and shapes of the tattoos could no longer be made out. Anna smiled at him.

'That's looking great, Callum. You've obviously been taking good care of it.'

'Yeah. Can we do some more now?'

Anna laughed. 'When the inflammation's gone right down. We'll book an appointment soon.'

'Great.' Callum turned to Jamie. 'Shall I go with Freddie?'

'Yep, that would be great.' Jamie turned his attention back to the chart, while Callum sauntered over to a young boy in a wheelchair, who was sitting on one side. The two exchanged a high-five and Callum pushed the wheelchair onto the court.

'Callum with *two* "l"s.' A girl of around seventeen with orange hair and a matching sweatshirt was looking over Jamie's shoulder.

'Ah. Yes.' Jamie squinted at the chart and then passed it over to the girl. 'Do me a favour, Jen…'

The girl nodded, and took over, writing everyone's names in the positions that Jamie assigned to them. Jamie clearly didn't mind asking for help here, and Anna guessed that it was all part of the culture amongst the group. Everyone helped everyone else.

'You said I could play…' She tugged at Jamie's sleeve, and he turned, smiling.

'I didn't forget. We're going to have a throw-around first, though. You might like to sit that out, to get an idea of the rules.'

Something told her that the rules probably weren't in any book. Anna nodded, walking over to one of the benches by the side of the court as the teams took up their positions. A middling-sized boy in glasses blew the whistle that hung around his neck, and play started.

It didn't make a lot of sense to Anna. The team captains were engaged in their own private tussle for the ball, but when it was passed to a younger child, they stood back. There was a group of mothers standing on the other side of the court, and Anna wondered whether she might go and introduce herself and ask for an explanation.

'Hi. I'm Jen.' The girl with the orange hair had made a beeline for where she was sitting, and sat down next to her. On the other side they were joined by a girl with heavy black make-up around her eyes, dyed black hair and a black sweatshirt.

'Hi, I'm Anna.'

'Yes, we know. That's Spark.' Jen gestured towards her companion. The two girls were sitting close on either side of her, and Anna had the feeling that she'd been ambushed. Maybe they were the two head girls in the group, and had decided to let her know about it.

'You came with Jamie?' Spark fixed her with a not-too-welcoming look.

'Yes, I work with him.'

'In London?' This time Jen asked the question.

'Yes, that's right.'

The two girls exchanged looks. Clearly this *was* an ambush of some kind.

'You're going out with him?' Jen asked.

Spark gave a knowing nod. 'Out here on a Sunday morning? They're going out.'

'No, we're just friends.'

Jen flashed her a disbelieving look. 'Okay, if that's the way you want it. Just friends.'

How did you explain the difference between pretending you were just friends and *being* just friends? Jen and Spark had clearly decided the question between themselves, and Anna had to admit that Spark had a point. Being here this early on a Sunday morning did raise a few questions about the nature of her relationship with Jamie.

She wondered what Jamie would have wanted her to say, and the answer came straight away. Be honest. Anna took a breath.

'You know, the kind of just friends where you're really going out together but you don't want anyone to know.'

Jen's lips curved in an expression of triumph. 'Yeah, we know.'

'Well, Jamie and I aren't that kind of just friends. We're really just friends.'

'Oh.' Jen gave her a searching look and Anna returned her gaze. Clearly that convinced her and she nodded. 'Well, we just thought...'

'And you decided to look me over?' Anna smiled. That was okay. It was actually quite nice that the girls cared enough to do it, however challenging they seemed.

'We didn't much like the other one, did we?' Spark wrinkled her nose.

Jen shook her head. 'Nah. She turned out to be a nasty piece of work.'

'He never gave her a sweatshirt.'

'Just as well. She didn't play… And after what she did, I'd have ripped it off her back.' Jen's lip curled.

'You and whose army?' Spark gave her friend a dismissive look. 'You were going to get on a plane and find her, were you?'

'Wait…' Anna shouldn't interfere, but she wanted to know. 'You know what happened?'

'Yeah, 'course we do.' Spark rolled her eyes. 'She went off with his brother. Jamie looked proper sorry for himself for a while.'

'He told you about it?'

'No, we saw pictures of them on the internet. Jamie didn't say anything.' Jen wrinkled her nose. 'We made him fairy cakes.'

'Oh. Well, it was nice of you to go to the trouble…'

'We *bought* the cakes,' Spark corrected her friend. 'Then we iced them. I put black icing and a skull and crossbones on mine. He didn't want to talk about it, but I reckon he got the message.'

'Yes, I expect he did.' Anna wasn't so sure, but the girls meant well. 'I'm sure it cheered him up.'

The ref's whistle sounded, and she looked up at the players. Jamie had turned towards the bench, and he frowned suddenly. 'Hey. Spark, Jen, aren't you playing?' Clearly he recognised an ambush when he saw one.

'Nah, we're explaining to the rules to your *friend*.' Jen's words didn't seem to reassure him at all and he shot Anna a questioning look.

'We won't be a minute. I think I'm getting the hang of this,' Anna called across to him, and he nodded, turning back to the other players.

'So what *are* the rules, then?'

Jen grinned. Clearly Anna had proved herself with the girls. 'You can only try and get the ball if the person who's already got it is the same size as you. You can pass it to someone who's bigger or smaller, but you can't take it from anyone smaller than you.'

Anna frowned. 'Doesn't that mean that those two bigger boys just hog the ball to themselves, though?'

Spark shook her head. 'You *have* to pass the ball, and you get extra points depending on who you pass it to. Don't worry about that, the ref works it out. Just don't throw the ball to Jamie or the team captains and you'll be fine. Everyone else is smaller than you.'

'Ah. I see. I think…' Anna watched as the teams started playing again. It was all making a bit more sense now.

'You'll get the hang of it.' Jen stood up. 'You wanna play?'

'Yes, thank you. I'd like to very much.' If Anna could survive Jen and Spark's interrogation tactics, she reckoned that the Hastings Hustlers basketball rules would be a breeze.

Jamie had shot her another querying glance when she walked onto the court with Jen and Spark, and she'd ignored it. Anna was beginning to enjoy herself. It was just a matter of passing the ball to as many different players as possible, so that the little kids could catch it and play too. Easy.

A howl went up as a little boy ran across to Jamie, clutching the ball to his chest, and threw it up towards him. Jamie hadn't touched the ball yet, preferring to run up and down and encourage the others, but the ref's whistle sounded in a signal that everyone should back off and give him a turn.

'No-o-o-o!' Jen's shout echoed across the court, and when Anna looked round she saw both Jen and Spark flapping their arms in her direction. 'Get him!'

Fair enough. Anna ran towards Jamie, and he deftly avoided her. She ducked under his arm, turning to block his path, and saw him smile. He was quick, and his reach was longer than hers, but she was quicker…

She managed to tip the ball from his grasp, but after a few bounces he got it back. She heard Jen and Spark howling with disappointment and redoubled her efforts. Finally she managed to get the ball and break free of him, bouncing the ball as she ran madly for the hoop.

Just as she slowed, ready to take her shot, he caught her, lifting her up off the ground and over his shoulder. Anna kept a tight hold on the ball as he walked back towards the other end of the court. The ref's whistle peeped frenetically, and Jamie ignored it.

'Cheat!'

She managed to get the word out through clenched teeth. Jamie was holding her tightly, and she resisted the temptation to kick him. Any minute now she was going to drop the ball and slide down into his arms, and that wouldn't do. Particularly after she'd just been at such pains to make it crystal clear what kind of *just friends* they were.

He reached the other end of the court and put her down, his green eyes full of mischief. The ref jogged up to him, and he backed off, grinning, as the boy waved his arms.

'Penalty!' The ref clearly took his responsibilities very seriously. 'And you're benched, Jamie. Ten minutes.'

Jamie took his punishment without question. Anna only just heard his murmured words as he walked past her.

'It was worth it.'

'Watch this.' Anna pulled a face at him, walking back to the other end of the court. She stopped well short of the place where he'd picked her up, in a spot behind the three-point line. Gauging the distance carefully, she reckoned she could make it. Jamie was sitting on one of the park benches now, shaking his head and motioning her closer to the hoop.

Everyone was watching to see what she'd do. Whether she could make the shot. Anna looked round and saw Spark, who gave her a thumbs-up sign. That was it. She *had* to make the shot now.

There was silence as the ball arced through the air. And then a howl of applause from both teams as it bounced against the backboard and through the hoop. Jen and Spark both careened towards her, hugging her and slapping her on the back.

'You trashed him…' Jen gestured towards Jamie, who was on his feet, applauding with all the others, seemingly unaware of his complete humiliation. The ref peeped his whistle, motioning everyone back to their places.

She was on the team now.

* * *

'So what were Spark and Jen saying to you?' Jamie had a feeling that the two girls had been doing a little more than just explaining the rules to Anna. The two of them could be difficult at times, but Anna had seemed to take it all in her stride.

'Oh, just girl talk.' She climbed into his car, smiling at him.

Heaven help him. Anna was ferocious enough on her own, and Jamie wasn't quite sure how to view a potential alliance between her and the girls.

'That was a hell of a shot.'

Anna grinned at him. 'Wasn't it exactly what you wanted me to do?'

Maybe not quite. The Hastings Hustlers were a tight-knit group, and while they welcomed other teens in their number they could be wary of adults, who they saw as authority figures. He'd reckoned a little outrageous cheating might break the ice and get them on Anna's side, and it had. But she'd outdone him.

'It didn't occur to me you were a basketball aficionado.'

'I played a lot of netball at school and it's

not so different.' Anna grinned at him. 'And the ref did a pretty good job of putting you in your place.'

Jamie chuckled. 'Yeah, Andrew's a good kid. He's our chess player and he doesn't much like running around with a ball, but he's a great referee. Very impartial and he knows all the rules by heart.'

He leaned forward, twisting the key in the ignition. 'What do you fancy for lunch? There's a great fish and chip restaurant down by the promenade.'

'Sounds good. I'm hungry.'

The fish and chip restaurant had a fifties vibe, with shining chrome, tiled walls and red leather seats. They found a table by the window, and a waitress with a check apron came to take their order, putting a carousel with red sauce, brown sauce, salt, vinegar and cutlery down onto the table.

Anna was staring out at the iron-grey sky, which merged into an iron-grey sea. It was starting to rain, and people were hurrying past, anxious to get out of the biting wind.

'So you got on pretty well with Jen and

Spark.' What Jamie *really* wanted to know was what the girls had been saying to Anna, but that had already been asked and answered.

'You just can't let it alone, can you?' She grinned at him.

'I'm just…' Jamie shrugged. He was actually just being protective, but Anna wouldn't like that. 'Just curious. They have their own agenda sometimes.'

'Oh, they definitely had an agenda. They'd decided that I was your girlfriend and that they'd give me a once-over to make sure I was good enough for you.'

Jamie winced. 'Ouch. Sorry…'

'That's okay. I thought it was rather sweet of them.' She paused, drawing circles with her finger on the tablecloth. 'Did you realise that they knew about what happened when you broke up with your fiancée?'

'What! No.' Jamie felt the hairs on the back of his neck suddenly spring to attention. 'I never mentioned it. I didn't want anyone to know.'

'Well, they're teenagers. They know how to use the internet. What Jon does and who he's with tends to get photographed and reported.' Anna's expression softened suddenly. 'And they said that you'd seemed upset about somcthing.'

'And I thought I was doing so well.'

She shot him a look that made his heart melt. If he'd known Anna then, he'd never have been able to keep silent.

'No one can hide a broken heart. Particularly not from a bunch of kids. They see what's going on a lot better than adults do.'

'Yeah, I guess so. Especially *these* kids. A lot of them have good reason to be watchful, they've been let down by the people around them.'

He didn't dare ask what Spark and Jen had thought about it all. What Anna had thought. When she brushed her fingers against the back of his hand, he knew exactly what she thought. Anna was there for him in a way that he couldn't have expected.

'They said they bought you fairy cakes. They wanted to make you feel better.'

'Fairy cakes?' Jamie thought back. 'Oh, yes, I remember now. They had enough for the whole team, and they gave me a bag to take home with me. They had black icing…'

A lump rose suddenly in his throat. He'd felt so alone then. If he'd just opened his eyes and seen, he'd have known that he hadn't been.

'There's nothing that says *Cheer up, we've got your back* quite like black icing and a skull and crossbones.' Anna grinned. 'I hope you got that message.'

'I suppose I did, in general terms. I remember thinking it was very nice of them, and that things couldn't be that bad after all.' A thought occurred to Jamie. 'They told you all this?'

'I generally find that when people ambush me for information it's because they're worried about something. If I tell them what they want to know, in plain and simple terms, then they respond to that and tell me what's bothering them. Jen and Spark think a lot of you, and they don't want to see you hurt again.'

Jamie was overwhelmed. No thought, just the feeling that there was so much he'd missed. So much he'd got wrong.

'I've been a fool, haven't I?'

Anna shook her head. 'I don't think so.'

The waitress arrived with their plates, and he took cutlery from the carousel, and then some tartare sauce to go with his fish. He watched as

Anna shook the bottle of tomato sauce, dribbling some onto her plate, then dipping one of her chips into it. Everything she did was enchanting, and it seemed that she was all he had to hold onto.

'Great chips.' She gave him a smile that seemed achingly intimate. As if she knew all his secrets and she didn't judge him for them. She just wanted to eat chips with him on a wet, windy day and watch the sea.

'I think… I could have done a few things differently.'

'You're in good company. You, me and everyone else on the planet.' She put another chip into her mouth, but she was watching him steadily.

'I could do a few things differently in the future, then.'

Anna smiled. 'That's a bit more to the point. The future's something we can change.'

'I've been thinking that the business with Jon and Gill was just one thing, and that it came out of the blue. It happened and I could keep it to myself, and control it.'

'And you've learned differently.'

'Well, clearly there were a few issues that

had been brewing before that. And I wasn't in control, I couldn't just keep going without anyone noticing.' Jamie thought for a moment. 'Maybe I should mention that to my counsellor.'

'What, that you're not completely in control of everything?' Anna gave him a knowing look.

'I sat down with her last week, and outlined the way I expected it all to go.' He allowed himself a rueful smile. 'What the issues were, and how I was going to resolve them.'

'I'll bet she just loved that. Where's the job satisfaction in counselling someone who's already got everything worked out?' Anna was teasing now.

'Yeah, okay. Just don't stop giving me a hard time, will you?'

'Of course not. That's what friends are for, isn't it?'

Jamie nodded. Being friends with Anna was so much more than he'd dared hope. And suddenly he had an appetite for the food in front of him. He picked up his knife and fork and began to eat.

CHAPTER TEN

WHEN ANNA'S PHONE had beeped yesterday, she'd thought that Jamie had just sent a message wishing her a good Monday morning after a weekend that had been so full of different emotions. He *had* done so, but the purpose of contacting her had been something else entirely. Something she'd been dreading.

She knew that Jamie had taken an interest in the abandoned baby that had been brought to the hospital two weeks ago. So much so that the nurses on the paediatric ward had named the little boy *James*. Anna had visited him once more, but had then stayed away, knowing that this day was going to come.

It wasn't until she'd arrived at work on Tuesday morning that she realised she'd dressed for the occasion. A dark skirt and jacket with high heels wasn't her usual style as she preferred the more informal look of a bright top with trousers. But today the distance of formality was her only armour.

'Hi. You okay?' Jamie seemed much the same as always. Tall and broad, deliciously handsome, and seeming to notice everything about her. *That* wasn't what she wanted to think about either.

'Yes, fine.' Anna pressed her lips into a determined line. 'I've got a pretty full schedule today, so…' Don't stop and talk. Just get it over with and leave.

'We'll make it quick, then. They're in one of the family rooms.' Jamie got the message, starting to walk purposefully towards the paediatric unit.

'Have they found the mother?' They stood alone in the lift together, and Anna couldn't help but ask.

'Yeah. She's very young and the social workers say that she wants to go ahead and have the baby adopted. Apparently everyone's in agreement that it'll be the best way forward for both mum and baby.'

Anna swallowed hard. 'So the couple we're seeing today…?'

'They're foster parents for the time being, but

they've been on the adoption list for a while, waiting to be matched with a child. If everything goes to plan, and I'm sure it will, they'll adopt James.'

Anna thought she saw a hint of pride in his face. A baby named after him. That was what any man wanted, wasn't it? 'Do they like the name the nurses gave him?'

Jamie shrugged, and the lift doors opened. 'What's not to like about it?'

His version of hurrying was to give the smiling impression that he had all the time in the world but still get straight to the point. Anna was introduced to Marianne and Neil, and she sat down, trying not to notice the glow in both their faces as they looked at the baby in Marianne's arms.

'I understand you'd like to know what the operations for syndactyly are going to entail.'

'Yes.' Marianne tore her gaze from the baby, and nodded her head. 'Whatever it takes, we'll be there for him. We'd just like to know how we can best care for him.'

Anna nodded. 'Well, the good news is that there's no reason why his fingers shouldn't be separated successfully. It'll take some time, and I'd advise you to discuss all the options with your surgeon. There are a number of centres of excellence that specialise in syndactyly.'

Neil nodded, reaching across to stroke little James's hand with his finger. 'We've seen the list you sent, thank you. He's perfect as he is, but we know that surgery can give him a lot more than he has at the moment, and we want to make sure we do things right.'

That was a great start. Anna reached into her bag, pulling out the information folder that she'd put together and handing it to Neil.

'I've got some fact sheets and a few web addresses for you. I'll just run through some of the main points, and then I know you have some questions for me...'

'Nice people.' Jamie had walked Marianne and Neil out to the entrance of the paediatric unit, holding the door open as they manoeuvred the new pram through it. Anna had hung back.

'Yes.'

'He's going to a good home. He'll be fine.'

Anna wanted to retort that he had no way of knowing that. But Marianne and Neil had been through the demanding process of being accepted as potential adoptive parents, and everything had been done to make sure that baby James would have all the care he deserved. Jamie had just picked up on her mood and was trying to reassure her. Maybe himself, too.

'Yes, you're right. He'll be fine.'

'So…you need to be getting back?'

She'd said that, hadn't she? And now she was standing, staring dumbly at the door, as if Marianne and Neil were going to bring baby James back for one last hug. The one that Anna hadn't dared give him.

'Yes, I do.' Anna smiled briskly up at him. 'Will I see you on Thursday?'

'I'll be there.'

'Good. I'll remember to clear a space on my desk for you.' Anna shouldered her bag, and walked away.

As she hurried through the main reception area of the hospital, she saw Marianne and Neil again, with an older couple who were bending over the pram. Probably baby James's new grandparents, who hadn't been able to wait to get a glimpse of him. Thankfully they didn't see her, and Anna made for the doors as fast as she could go without careening into someone.

Marianne and Neil were embarking on a journey that Anna would have loved to take. She'd begged Daniel to take it with her, but he'd refused, saying he wanted his own biological children. Anna hadn't tried to persuade him any further. Daniel had already changed his mind about not wanting children, and had left her. They would never have been the kind of couple that could look after an adopted child, the way that Marianne and Neil were.

She should just forget all about it. Baby James would be well cared for. If it seemed that he'd left a gaping hole in her life, it was only because that hole had always existed and was never going to be filled. Not with anyone, least of all Jamie.

Anna had become attached to baby James. That wasn't in the least surprising, the little boy's happy temperament belying his difficult start in life, and he'd been a favourite amongst everyone at the hospital. Jamie had got a little too attached himself, but he knew that everything was being done to make sure that both the baby and his biological mother were being properly cared for.

All the same, her reaction had puzzled him. He could have understood if she'd given him a hug and brushed away a tear, the way that the paediatric nurses had done. But Anna had been clearly struggling to hold her feelings back, and that piqued his curiosity. Anna was generally in the habit of telling him exactly what was on her mind.

Maybe she'd got to thinking about the kiss, and had decided it had been inappropriate. But she greeted him with a smile when he arrived at the clinic on Thursday, and the brush of her fingers on his arm told him that she was thinking nothing of the sort. Which was just fine, because Jamie didn't regret it either.

'We're playing baseball on Sunday morning.'

They'd been sitting in silence, both concentrating on the papers in front of them on Anna's desk. Actually, Anna had given every appearance of concentrating on her paperwork, while Jamie had been wrestling with how to phrase his invitation.

'Yes?' She looked up at him. 'I heard that the forecast was for rain over the weekend.'

He'd heard that too. And if getting thoroughly cold and wet with Anna seemed like a taste of heaven to him, he didn't blame her for finding it an unenticing prospect.

'I should probably book an inside court.'

'Yes, probably.' Her gaze shifted to the papers in front of her again.

This wasn't going quite the way he'd planned. Anna had sensed his ulterior motive and was already backing away from it. He should have been a great deal clearer about what he was asking of her.

'Jon's going to be staying with Caroline this weekend. I'm going to leave them to it, and was wondering if you're free…' Anna didn't look up at him, but Jamie lapsed into silence as he saw the tops of her ears redden.

'Jamie. Don't embarrass me…'

He hadn't meant to. And the only way that this could embarrass her was if she was about to say no. He liked spending time with Anna, and he knew that she liked spending time with him, but they both needed the reassurance of having a reason to be together. Just wanting to be together wasn't enough.

Without looking at him, Anna picked up her

pen again and started to write. The tops of her ears were still burning red, and the silence in the room was pressing down on him like a ten-ton weight.

Long minutes passed. Her phone was going to ring any moment now, calling her away, or it would be time for him to go and visit Jon's room to have lunch with him. The subject of seeing Anna again would have been dropped, and with every moment that passed it would become increasingly unlikely that it would ever be broached again.

'Look, Anna. Neither of us has any plans for a relationship right now. So could we take that off the table, please?' Jamie blurted the words out.

She looked up at him. Then she smiled. It was a little watery, but it was a smile all the same.

'Yes. You're right, we should do that.'

'So keeping that firmly in mind… I'd like to be your friend and spend some time with you.'

She thought for a moment. 'I'd like that too. I'm free at the weekend.'

The weight lifted from his shoulders and

Jamie suddenly felt as light as a feather. 'That's great. I am too, so maybe we could do something together.'

Now that a relationship had been taken off the table, it had allowed everything else to be added. Jamie had mentioned that the trees in the orchard were laden with fruit, ready to be harvested, and Anna had suggested they do it together. They'd driven down late on Friday evening, only giving themselves time for a nightcap before he went to his bedroom and she went to hers.

Jamie had slept peacefully for the first time in weeks, just knowing that she was in the house, even if he couldn't hold her. In the morning, he'd cooked breakfast, and they'd walked down to the orchard together, Anna carrying the boxes for the apples and Jamie taking the sturdy ladder that would be needed to reach the highest branches.

'I think that's about it…' They'd gathered up the windfalls, and sorted the apples into two boxes, ones that were perfect and those that were damaged.

'There are still some on that tree, over there.'

Jamie shook his head. 'They're not ready to pick yet.'

'Just as well probably. What are you going to do with all these?' Anna gestured towards the four large boxes of apples.

'Um… Caroline will take some of them. And I can pack the undamaged ones and put them in the outhouse, they'll keep for a while.'

Anna nodded. 'What about picking some blackberries and making pies with the windfalls? You could freeze them.'

'Good idea.' There hadn't been so many apples last year, and Jamie had given them all to Caroline, because making pies would have reminded him that he'd had no one to eat them with. Now it felt like a *real* harvest.

He carted the boxes back to the house while Anna picked blackberries. Two boxes were set aside for Caroline, and Jamie put the box of windfalls on the kitchen table.

'Do we have enough?' Anna surveyed the apples and blackberries, and Jamie laughed.

'Enough for what? How many people were you thinking of feeding?'

'I meant enough butter and flour for pastry.'

Jamie opened the refrigerator, pulling out half a packet of butter. 'No, I guess not.'

'We'd better get some, then.'

Going to the supermarket felt like an excursion to heaven. Weaving through Saturday shoppers with a trolley, standing patiently as Anna changed her mind for the third time about how much flour they'd need, and then loading everything into the car. Stopping for coffee and a sandwich on the way home, because they had too much to do this afternoon to contemplate cooking lunch. He'd done this a thousand times, and it had slipped past him like all the other irrelevancies in life. Today it felt special.

'How are you at pastry-making?' Her face was shining as they re-entered the kitchen. Anna was enjoying herself too, and that made it all perfect.

'I can give it a try. Caroline does it all the time, it doesn't look too difficult.'

Anna grinned at him. 'I'll make the first batch of pastry then, and you can make a start on peeling the apples.'

When it was Jamie's turn to make the pastry, he found that it wasn't as easy as either Caroline or Anna made it look. But practice seemed to be the key ingredient, and after a few false starts Anna judged his pastry good enough to line some of the foil pie dishes they'd bought.

'The counselling's going well…' He was still curious about the things that Anna didn't talk about, and it seemed to Jamie that if he were candid with her, it might encourage a similar response.

'Yes?' She grinned at him. 'That's good.'

'My counsellor said she was relieved to find that *I* wasn't going to be billing *her*.'

Anna snorted with laughter, dropping the apple she was peeling into the basin of water in front of her. It landed with a plop, scattering water all over the table. 'I'd be wanting to get that one sorted out as well.'

'Yeah. We've made the demarcation lines a bit clearer. These sessions are part of a learning process for *me*, not the other way round.'

'It's a bit of an occupational hazard, I suppose. When you're so used to counselling the kids in your care.'

Jamie chuckled. 'Thanks for letting me off the hook. Although I suspect it's a bit more to do with the fact that I reckoned that it was all about what Gill and Jon did, and that I didn't bear any of the blame for what happened.'

'I'm sure your counsellor didn't say *blame*, did she?' Anna was mopping up the water on the table.

'No, you're quite right, she didn't. She said *responsibility*. More flour?'

'Yes, just sprinkle a bit more on the board before you roll it out. It'll stop it sticking… So what areas of responsibility have you owned up to? If you don't mind my asking.'

'No, of course not.' Jamie thought back through the twisted strands of everything that had happened, and the beginning of it all seemed very clear now. 'Gill and I met on a train. She was sitting opposite me, staring at me, and finally she asked if I was Jonny Campbell. Jon and I looked a bit more alike in those days.'

'Oh…' Anna's face twisted into pained expression.

'Yeah, I know. It's ironic, but… Actually, that just about sums it all up. We started talking, and laughed about it a bit, and I dismissed the idea that she'd actually rather I was Jon. But, looking back, I think she always wondered if he might be a bit more exciting than I am.'

'That's not very fair. You're exciting.'

The way she flew to his defence was nice to hear. 'Not quite in the way Jon is. Gill liked to go out a lot, the fancier the place the better. She didn't have a lot of time for the work I do with the charity, she rather felt that got in the way. She made no bones about the fact that I could be a bit boring about it sometimes.'

'She sounds a bit boring herself.' Anna winced at her own reaction. 'Sorry. I didn't mean to be rude. I don't even know her.'

'I appreciate the vote of confidence. Gill and I were just different. I had what I really wanted, and when there were conflicting claims on my time, I chose the charity over her. She was right to leave me.'

'Not in that way, Jamie.'

'No. Not in that way.' He shrugged. None of that seemed to matter so much now. 'So what about you?'

'Me?' Anna was suddenly uncomfortable, and it struck Jamie that she was just pretending not to know what he meant.

'I've appreciated the way you've encouraged me to talk. Can't I return the favour?'

Anna shook her head quickly. It seemed she wasn't even going to consider the idea. 'It is what it is. I've nothing to talk about and…so I don't.'

'I'm always here. If you change your mind.'

'Yeah. Thanks.' Something about the finality of her tone told Jamie that she wasn't going to change her mind. 'Oh, look out! You've got a hole…'

Jamie looked down at the pastry in front of him, and saw he'd rolled it a little too thin. Anna nudged him out of the way, folding the pastry over deftly so that he could try again and dusting the board with flour. The moment was gone.

Fair enough. If she didn't want to talk then he shouldn't press the point. He turned his attention to rolling out the pastry, and together they filled the rest of the foil pie dishes.

'Perhaps we should mark those three.' Anna pointed to the pies made with Jamie's pastry. He chuckled.

'With a skull and crossbones? Eat at your peril?'

'No! Your first home-made, home-grown apple and blackberry pies. You need to know when you're eating them.' She pulled a face, deftly cutting three capital J's from the scraps of pastry on the counter, and sticking them down on the top of the pies with a splash of water.

'Do we get to bake them all now?' The idea of filling the house with the scent of baking seemed suddenly thrilling. As if he was making a new start, in a new home.

'No, I think it's better to freeze them unbaked. We could keep one back to have tonight, though.'

'Sounds good. I'll do the washing up and then lay a fire in the sitting room…'

CHAPTER ELEVEN

PICKING APPLES AND making pies. Right now Anna couldn't think what might make a day better. But in truth it wasn't any of that which had made her day perfect. It was Jamie.

They sat on either side of the large grate, eating apple pie and cream. It tasted so much better made with apples that had still been on the tree this morning. Jamie laid his empty plate to one side.

'I'm not sure that even I can manage a third helping.'

'No. Neither can I.' Her stomach was full, and she was warm and relaxed after a day's work. They'd achieved something that might not be as important as the challenges they both met every day at work but it was more clear-cut. A task that had been started and finished, without any of the loose ends that medical treatment had a habit of presenting.

And now… He was so handsome in the fire-light.

Anna bit her lip. She had no business thinking such things, it was way beyond the terms of their agreement. And it was that agreement that allowed her to be here, the one that stipulated that spending time together was just that, and not the precursor to something that neither of them could consider.

'Maybe we should think about making cider next year.'

We. Next year.

That was a promise that couldn't be kept if they strayed past the boundaries they'd set.

'Yes, that sounds…interesting. Do you know how to make cider?'

Jamie shook his head. 'Not a clue. There's a first time for everything.'

She got to her feet, reaching for the empty plate that lay next to him on the table. Maybe walking out into the kitchen and washing up would shake the spell that seemed to have settled around them.

'Leave that…' Jamie reached out, catching her hand. In the firelight it was impossible to tell what colour his eyes were, but she could still see everything that mattered in them.

'I had a really nice day today. Thank you.' Anna could hear her voice tremble. One move from him, and she'd forget everything she'd been telling herself.

'So did I. Thank *you.*' He was leaning forward, raising her hand slowly to his lips. Every moment seemed laced with powerful magic.

He made just one, gentle movement. She could have taken her hand from his and resisted him easily. It was her own desire that pulled her down, and that welcomed the feeling of his arms around her. But sitting on his lap, curled in front of the fire was just too delicious.

'This is nice.' Jamie's chest rose and fell, as if he'd been starved for air for a long time and finally he could take a breath.

'Yes.' She curled her fingers around his. 'Not what we agreed, though.'

'We both said that we didn't want a relationship. I don't recall us mentioning any rules for our friendship.'

'Oh! So you've found a loophole, have you?' She dug her fingers playfully into his ribs.

'Not so much a loophole. Something that wasn't originally covered.'

'That's exactly what a loophole is,' Anna protested, although she still didn't move. 'Although…you're right. We never did define what kind of friendship we'd have.'

He chuckled quietly. 'Maybe we should thrash out the terms of that agreement in more detail. Clearly we need a more rigorous negotiating stance.'

And Anna had the perfect opening gambit. Moving in his arms, she turned to face him, leaving only inches between his lips and hers. 'No talking about the future, Jamie.'

'Agreed. You want it in writing?'

'No. This'll do.' She brushed her lips against his and heard him catch his breath.

'Anything else?'

'We're friends first. We don't need to be joined at the hip, and we can respect each other's lives.'

'That sounds more than fair.' He caught her hand, pressing her fingers to his lips. Then he kissed her palm, working his way across to the base of her thumb. Anna felt herself start to tremble.

'Anything else that happens is…'

'Entirely a matter between ourselves?' His eyes darkened suddenly. Maybe it was a trick of the light, but the way his body felt against hers was no trick.

'Yes.'

He was still and silent for a moment, staring into her eyes. Everything that she wanted was right there. She kissed him and his tender response couldn't completely hide his hunger.

'Stop me, if I go too far…'

'You're not going far enough, Jamie.'

His hands moved. One rested at the back of her head and the other began to explore. It was a slow, agonising expedition into just how much pleasure a moment could contain, and Jamie was watching her silently. When he cupped her breast, his thumb moving across the fabric of her shirt, she caught her breath.

'Oh!' The agony of frustration was only bearable because she knew now that she wasn't going to allow him to stop.

'You're so beautiful.' He kissed her cheek and she felt it burn. Slowly, deliberately he undid the buttons of her shirt. His fingers traced the edge of her bra, straying across her breast, and she gasped. He was drinking in her pleasure, his eyes fixed on her face.

She wanted his pleasure, too. And she wanted to tease it from him slowly. She wriggled out of his embrace, backing away from him and slipping out of her shirt as she did so. Anna felt the warmth of the fire against her skin as she undressed, the heat of his gaze as he watched her.

'Come here.' She crooked her finger and he was on his feet in an instant. Anna took her time about unbuttoning his shirt, sliding her hands across his shoulders, feeling his heart thundering in his chest.

'Anna…!' He groaned out loud as she ran her tongue across his nipple, so she did it again. He was so strong and yet so entirely in her power. And then when his gaze swept hungrily across her body, she was entirely in his power.

Finally they were naked. This was so much more than just lust, it was loving friends who wanted to see everything. Feel everything, before the inevitable climax robbed them of this trembling anticipation.

When they embraced, she felt the tautness of his body against hers. Then he fell to his knees, one hand still pinioning her tightly against him, the other sliding between her legs. She felt his mouth against her breast, and she cried out, hanging onto his shoulders.

'Too much?' His eyes shone teasingly in the firelight as he looked up at her.

'Not enough, Jamie. It's not enough...' She gasped as she felt his arms around her sweeping her off her feet and lowering her to the floor.

The hearth rug was warm against her back. In the heat of the moment all she wanted was to feel him inside her, but Jamie had other ideas. His hands and his mouth were everywhere, and she cried out as he pulled her legs apart. He was pushing her close to her limit, and she felt a bead of sweat run across her brow, then further, past her limits, to a place where she responded only to his touch.

Then he slowed. She felt his weight on her, and she wrapped her legs around him, desperate for the sweet friction of his body against hers.

'More...please...' She'd never begged a man before, but that didn't seem to matter right now.

'More?' There was something steely in his

gaze. It told her that he could break her, and that was exactly what she wanted him to do. Break her and then hold her tight, before he did it all over again.

'Jamie! Please…' Her fist beat weakly against his shoulder, and he moved. Running his fingers from her neck to her navel, then right back where she wanted them. He was searching for the exact place that gave her the most pleasure, looking for clues in her face. When he found it, his lips curved in triumph.

A little faster. A little more pressure. She guided him as best she could, but he didn't need much help. He seemed to know when it was just perfect, and lifted his weight a little to allow her body to arch under his. When she felt his lips touch her nipple she came. So hard, so quickly. Maybe she screamed, maybe not. When she stilled and wrapped her arms around him, she felt a long sigh rack his body.

'You are amazing.' He rolled over onto his back, pulling her on top of him.

'Me? You were the one who seemed to be doing all the work.' She snuggled against him. 'Although don't think you're going to get away without doing a little more. Do you have any condoms?'

'I'll find them.' He kissed her cheek, tenderly. 'Don't you want to rest a bit?'

No. Not now. It was warm in front of the fire, and she was comfortable here. But Jamie had awakened a rolling desire that hadn't been slaked and was fast gaining momentum again.

'I want to feel you inside me. You want that?' She moved against him and he gasped. He flexed his hips a little and his erection hardened against her leg.

'What do you think?'

When he picked her up, carrying her out into the hallway, the chilled air made her shiver. His bedroom door was opposite that of the guest bedroom, and she'd only ever seen the outside of it. Jamie pushed it open, but she didn't much care to look around her, all she needed right now was him.

He laid her down on the bed and she felt the warmth of his body against hers as he leaned over to kiss her.

'Stay there. I won't be a moment...' She saw his shadow move and there was the sound of him opening and closing drawers. It was cold in here and Anna pulled the duvet over her. Jamie seemed to have found what he was looking for, and his shadow moved to the end of the bed. Then a large brick fireplace suddenly glowed into life as a gas fire ignited.

Flickering light filled the room, and his shadow was more substantial now as he moved towards her. Anna sat up, and he bent to kiss her again.

'You want warm and comfortable?' He tugged at the duvet, his mouth curving into a smile.

Warm and comfortable was nice. She wanted more than nice. 'What do you want?'

He leaned forward. 'I want to be able to see you, and for you to see me. I want to be what keeps you warm.'

Hot desire started to course though her veins. They could make use of every inch of the large bed, unencumbered by bedding. And she'd be able to see it all.

'That's what I want, too.' Her fingers tightened on the duvet, holding it firmly around her, and she leaned forward to kiss him. 'Take it…'

She heard his quiet laugh and then he wrested

the duvet from her grip. His hands were still cold and he was making full use of them to make her squirm and gasp under his touch. Suddenly she was on her back, Jamie's knees planted on either side of her hips. His hands closed gently around her wrists and she felt hot desire flooding through her body.

'I want you to take *me*, Jamie…'

His grip tightened, and he pinioned her arms above her head. Raking her body with his gaze, and then covering it with his. She wrapped her legs around him, and he kissed her mouth, hard and searching.

They were the same. They both took pleasure in moments of exquisite tenderness and the long, slow build-up of desire. Whispered words, waiting and watching to see the reaction to every new caress. But when passion got the better of them, she was bold. Unafraid to challenge him, and unafraid to *be* challenged.

Anna was his match. Equal and opposite forces, they fitted each other's desires perfectly.

Her hair glinted in the firelight, spread across the pillow. When he pushed gently inside her, she seemed to bloom under him, and Jamie was carried away by the sweet ebb and flow of her lovemaking. Suddenly strong, because she had no hesitation in showing him how much he pleased her.

Sweat trickled down his spine. Every muscle quivered at her touch, and when she pushed him over onto his back, he knew one thing for sure.

'I'm in real trouble now…'

'Yes, you are.' She bent over to kiss him. 'And you can't talk your way out of it…'

He knew. When Anna climbed astride him, taking him inside her again, it seemed that everything else was just a whisper in his imagination. Only she was real. She twisted her hips and he couldn't help crying out.

She bound him in sweet, silken bonds of pleasure. All he could see was Anna. She was all he could feel. Her pace quickened a little and he reached up to caress her body, knowing that she was close to breaking. He wanted to watch, but when he felt her muscles tighten around him he couldn't hold on any longer. He roared out her name, as his own release crashed over him.

It was a long time before he was able to speak. Jamie just held her, feeling her heart beat against his in a crazy rhythm. What they'd just done together had been frightening in its intensity, but he couldn't let her go.

'That was the very best kind of trouble.' He kissed her forehead.

'Mmm…' she agreed sleepily, snuggling against him.

All he wanted to do now was to hold her in his arms, feeling the soft rhythm of her breathing against his chest. He wanted to drift off to sleep and find her there when he woke up. And if this really *was* asking for trouble, a loophole in their agreement that neither of them should have opened, he didn't care. He'd worry about that later.

Jamie dreamed that he was caught in a web. Sticky and oleaginous strands held him fast, and every time he broke free there seemed to be more in every direction. He could hear Anna's breathing, feel it almost, and he knew that he had to protect her but he didn't know how. In the distance, an alarm was trilling. Something was wrong, and he had to get out.

'Jamie… Jamie!'

He came to suddenly, still locked in the folds of the dream. His alarm actually *was* sounding, on the bedside table, and Jamie reached over to silence it. Something got in his way, and he realised that Anna really was there, too.

'Uh… Sorry.'

'That's okay. You were dreaming?'

'Yes.' The alarm was still boring into his brain, but he'd have to lean across Anna to shut it off. Jamie realised that he was naked, and that she was too. That hadn't seemed like a problem last night…

This morning it was an obstacle for both of them. Wrapped firmly in the duvet, she slid across the bed, hitting the snooze button on the alarm. That was the first problem of the morning, and quite possibly the simplest.

'You have to go, don't you?'

That wouldn't have been so difficult if Anna hadn't echoed Gill's words. She'd seemed to like the fact that he was often on call at first, she'd said he must be important if everyone needed to call him so often. But after a while she'd frowned when his phone had rung in the middle of the night or at a dinner party, and

Jamie had even considered not answering a few times. But he *had* to answer. Each one of these calls could be a child in trouble, and he'd promised to be there for them, day or night.

'I'm sorry…' That was what he'd always said to Gill as well. This was turning into a re-run of old memories and old mistakes, and it was just what Jamie had been trying to avoid, for both their sakes.

'That's okay. We're not joined at the hip, you know. Remember?'

He did, and suddenly everything seemed okay. Better, at least. Anna had only been to basketball practice once, but she'd obviously enjoyed it, and become more involved than Gill ever had.

'I remember. But it's bad timing.'

Anna raised her eyebrows. 'Not really. I'd come with you, but…twice in a row…' She shrugged. 'You don't want everyone gossiping about you.'

'If it keeps them out of trouble, they can gossip all they like. If you want to come, then come. If you want to stay here and have a lazy morning, then I'll be sparing a few jealous thoughts for you.'

She flashed him a sudden smile. 'I've brought my sweatshirt, and it seems a shame not to use it. I'd love to come, thanks.'

That was the first thing settled, and the overwhelming dread that Jamie had felt when he'd woken was beginning to subside. Anna seemed less awkward and embarrassed too, but in order to get to the court, they had to get up. And under the covers that Anna was holding so firmly around her, they were still both naked.

He reached forward, touching her hand. After last night his reticence seemed laughable, but he thought he saw a flare of panic in Anna's eyes, too.

'Last night. I won't ever regret it, Anna.'

Her cheeks flushed a little. 'Neither will I. It was nice, wasn't it?'

'Nice doesn't really do it for me. Try amazing. I'm not forgetting what we said, and I don't presume to lay claim to you, or any of your time. But if you wanted to spend some more of it with me, I'd honoured.'

She leaned towards him, kissing his cheek. The duvet had slipped a little, and some of the madness of last night reasserted itself. Only it wasn't madness. In the cold light of day Anna was just as beautiful, and just as desirable.

'Thank you. I was a little worried and… Sorry…'

He laid his finger across her lips. 'Don't be. I don't want you to be sorry for anything, because I'm not.'

The duvet slipped a little more as she gave him a hug. Jamie could feel the softness of her skin against his, and he regretted having missed the feeling of waking up next to her in an embrace.

'I'm sorry for one thing. That we don't have time now…' She nodded towards the clock, ticking relentlessly on the table beside the bed.

Maybe he shouldn't. It was better to leave while they both still wanted more than to overstay his welcome. But that was ridiculous, wanting more couldn't be changed by whatever happened next.

'My alarm's set to go off twice. If I get up on the first ring, then I get breakfast. The second ring means I get coffee in the car…'

'The car's really the only place for coffee.'

He kissed her, pulling the duvet out from between their bodies. 'Yeah. My thoughts exactly.'

Sex was a great way to begin the day. Sex with Jamie…? What could go wrong on a day that had started in his embrace?

She'd feared that it would be so different. When she'd woken from a deep sleep, just ten minutes before the alarm started to sound, it had felt as if she'd messed everything up. Allowed her feelings for Jamie to get the better of her, and lost everything.

But he'd meant what he'd said last night. That they could be loving friends, and that he wouldn't ask her for anything more than that. It seemed too good to be true, but maybe she should just take her good fortune and make the most of it. If making the most of it meant another night in his arms, then the risk seemed paltry in the face of the rewards.

Their long, playful lovemaking last night, had taught him how to take her from nought to a hundred in sixty seconds flat. And Jamie clearly loved the challenge. He fed off her arousal, the way she fed off his, and it all just worked between them. Effortless beauty.

There was even time to snuggle against him afterwards. Quiet moments, when the world began to expand from the complete and blissful circle of his embrace.

'I like your room.' His bedroom was in the same style as the rest of the house. Bare walls that contrasted with the high polish on the wooden bedframe. A large, brick-built fireplace that had provided them with warmth and light in the darkness.

He grinned. 'Only just noticed?'

'I've had other things on my mind.'

'Yeah, me too. You're welcome back anytime to get a better look.' He followed her gaze to the metal post that ran from floor to ceiling in the middle of the deep bay window. 'That's not part of the overall plan. It's just temporary.'

'I was wondering. It doesn't seem either old enough or new enough to be here.'

Jamie chuckled. 'It's a jack post. There was originally a window seat in that bay, with a wooden beam that supported the ceiling in the centre. It was rotten and I had to take it out. I was planning on getting a carpenter in to redo the whole thing properly, but that's going to have to wait.'

'No time?'

'No money. Or, to be more accurate, it was a choice between doing that and laying a floor in the community room at the youth centre. I think the floor's been a little more useful, and in the meantime the post is stopping the ceiling from falling in.'

'Sounds like a good decision.' There was a lot to respect about a man who could put his charity first when he needed to.

'I thought so.' He turned the corners of his mouth down.

'Someone else disagreed?'

The alarm went off suddenly, and they both jumped. Jamie reached across, banging his hand rather harder than he needed to on the button at the top.

'Yeah, Gill did. But there's no need to talk about the past. Unless, of course, you want to talk about yours?'

'Mine's simple.' Anna climbed over him, getting out of the bed. 'I was married and it didn't work out. I don't want to repeat past mistakes.'

That was all she wanted to say. If she told Jamie the truth, maybe he'd swear it didn't matter to him that she couldn't have children. Maybe she'd believe him. And it would all too painful when he realised that he really did want to be a father, the way Daniel had.

Jamie flung himself back on the pillows in an expression of frustration. 'Nothing's that simple,' he called out after her as she made for the shower room and turned on the water.

'Can't hear you. And anyway we have to get going, or we'll be late.'

CHAPTER TWELVE

FOR ONCE, TIME was on Jamie's side, pushing him towards the weekend, when he'd see Anna again. Three incredibly busy days working in A and E had flown by. Thursday and Friday were spent at the clinic, and in between seeing Jon and sorting out various issues to do with the charity, Jamie was fully occupied. Anna was working on Saturday morning, then they drove down to Hastings together.

The call came just as they'd arrived in the car park of the local pub for a late lunch. Jamie looked at the caller display and frowned, then accepted the call.

'Hi, Philip. What's up?'

He listened carefully to whoever was at the other end of the line. Clearly something *was* up because his brow darkened.

'Okay, let me make a couple of calls. I'll let you know.' He ended the call, puffing out a breath as he turned to Anna.

'I'm sorry. I have to go.'

'What's happened?'

'It's Spark. She's gone missing. Her parents called Jen, apparently, and she says she doesn't know where she is.'

'You think she does?'

He quirked his lips down. 'Maybe. Let me try her.'

He flipped through the contacts list on his phone, leaning back against the car and putting the phone to his ear. He shook his head, ending the call and redialling.

'You can't get hold of her?'

'She's not answering.' Jamie frowned. 'Now I *know* something's up. Her best friend's missing and she's not answering her phone?'

He had a point. Jamie waited, ended the call and dialled a third time, staring up at the sky in a silent signal that he could do this for as long as it took until Jen answered her phone. Then he gave a brisk nod…

'Hey, Jen. It's Jamie. Where are you? Yeah, I can hear you're on the bus. Where's the bus?'

He listened to Jen's reply, rolling his eyes. 'Pull the other one, Jen. Spark's missing, today of all days, and you're going to the cinema?'

It was an approach. Maybe not the most tactful one, but Anna imagined that tact had already been tried. And Jamie's relationship with all the kids was honest. He told them what he thought, and they repaid the compliment.

'No, Jen. I'll take you wherever you want to go in the car, no questions asked. If Spark's not where you think she is, then we'll keep looking. Please don't do this on your own.'

He listened again, his face grave.

'No, it's not because I don't trust you. It's because this is too much responsibility for one person. In your place, I'd need someone with me…' Jen seemed to have capitulated because Jamie nodded. 'Okay. I'll meet you at the bus stop in Hedge Lane. Wait for me there, I'll be fifteen minutes.'

He ended the call and turned to Anna, a look of apology on his face. 'Um… I'll drop you off at my place. It's on the way…'

'You will not. I can help, can't I?'

Jamie smiled suddenly. 'Yeah. Thanks, you can help.'

'So what's going on?' She waited until he'd manoeuvred the car back out of the car park and was on the road.

'Spark's younger brother died of leukaemia four years ago. She started coming to the club when he was really ill, and she met Jen there and they became friends. Spark used to talk a lot about how her brother felt, and how her parents felt, but nothing about herself. She was all about looking after everyone else.'

'Oh, poor Spark. You got her to talk?'

'Eventually. It was a while before she'd even admit to feeling anything when her brother died. Jen really supported her, though she's got problems of her own, and she understood what Spark was going through. Even if Spark didn't tell Jen where she was going, I guessed she might have a good idea.'

'Why now?' Jamie had said *today of all days.*

'It's the fourth anniversary of her brother's death today. Maybe Spark's finally found some space in her head for her own grief.'

'Her parents must be beside themselves.'

'Yeah, they are. They called our weekend helpline, and Phil told them that we'd do all we could. I'd better get back to him…'

'Let me do that. You keep driving.' Anna picked up his phone from the dashboard. 'What do you want me to say?'

'Tell him that we're on our way to meet Jen to see if she knows anything. He's calling round to see if anyone else has seen her, and he'll liaise with the police and her parents.'

The car slowed suddenly as the lights up ahead of them turned red. Jamie cursed under his breath, tapping his finger impatiently on the steering wheel. More than anything, his reaction made her fear the worst.

It took them thirteen minutes. A bus that was travelling ahead of them stopped, and Anna saw Jen get off and slump down on a seat in the bus shelter. She was taking her phone out of her pocket as Jamie drew up alongside her. Anna opened the car door, getting out of the front seat and beckoning to Jen to take her place.

'Where to, Jen?' Jamie's voice was suddenly calm.

'The railway lines, up by the station.'

Railway lines? Anna climbed into the back seat of the car, trying not to betray her concern.

'Seat belt.' Jamie waited while Jen fumbled

with the seat belt, then started to drive. 'Why there?'

'Spark's brother was in hospital in London at the end. Her parents used to go down there to be with him and Spark stayed with her aunt.'

Jamie nodded. 'Yes, I remember. I went round there to see her a few times.'

'She used to go and watch the trains. I went there a couple of times with her. We never told anyone, she was just watching.'

'For her parents to come back?'

Jen shrugged. 'No, not really. We wouldn't have seen them even if they had been on the train. She said that she was at one end of the line and they were at the other, I guess it made her feel more connected to them. We just used to sit on the embankment for an hour and then go home.'

It was an intensely private and personal admission for Jen to make, and it showed the depth of trust that Jamie had built up with the kids that he tried to help. Two young girls, doing something that made no sense but somehow made them feel better. If only that something was in a slightly less isolated and safer place.

'Okay. So we'll start at the road bridge closest to Jen's aunt's house?'

'Yeah. I reckon so.'

Jamie drew up in the centre of a wide bridge, and before either of them could stop her Jen tumbled out of the car, running across the pavement to the high railings. Jamie turned in his seat.

'You'll keep an eye on her?'

His gaze met hers and Anna nodded. One second of contact, but she knew that he trusted her to look after Jen while he searched for Spark. Warmth flooded through her, and she got out of the car, hurrying over to Jen.

The three of them scanned the embankment on either side of the lines. Jen was crying now, and Jamie's face was impassive as he concentrated on looking for some trace of Spark.

'There!' Jen screamed, pointing to spot on the embankment to one side of the bridge. The small, black-clad figure was sitting almost under the bridge, with her legs drawn up to her chest, as if she was trying to make herself as small as possible. And she was heart-stoppingly close to the tracks.

Jamie didn't even look back. He started to

run and Jen went to follow him, but Anna grabbed her, pulling her back.

'Let me go…' Jen swore at her.

'Wait. Wait!' Anna held her tight, waiting for her to stop struggling. 'Listen to me, Jen. You need to calm down if you're going to help Spark.'

Jen gulped down her tears. She saw the sense in it, and the only thing she wanted now was to help her friend. Anna just had to convince her that maybe she wasn't the best person to do that, and that she should leave it to Jamie.

'Do you know how she got down there?' A high fence bordered the embankment, and Anna knew that Jamie was relying on her to try and find a way through for him.

'There's a hole. Just there, by those trees.' Jen indicated a spot close to the end of the bridge.

'Okay. He's nearly there…' Anna waited for Jamie to turn and look back at her, and he did so right on cue. She pointed towards the spot that Jen had indicated, and he vaulted across the low railings that separated the pavement from the rough ground beyond, sliding down the steep incline towards the fence.

'No...' Jen was gesturing furiously. 'Further along...'

Jamie saw her, and turned. Then he gave a thumbs-up signal and disappeared behind the clump of trees and bushes that Jen had pointed out.

'I've got to go... Let me *go!*' Jen started to pull away from her again.

'Jamie's nearly there now. He'll bring her back.'

'But you don't *understand.* She's not trying to kill herself.' Tears were streaming down Jen's face again.

'He knows. She's feeling so much pain right now, and she's just trying to find a way of expressing it. Jamie understands that.'

Jen wiped her face, calming suddenly. 'She cuts herself, too.'

Anna wondered if Jamie knew that. He must realise it was a possibility, and he'd be taking everything into consideration right now. She put her arm around Jen's shoulders and they watched as Jamie appeared, slithering down the steep slope of the embankment and then starting to walk towards Spark.

He stopped thirty feet away from her, and

must have called to her because Spark turned. His movements were slow and controlled, all his body language reassuring. He took a couple more steps then sat down on the grass.

He edged closer, stopping when Spark flailed one arm in his direction in a gesture that told him to back off. They seemed to be talking, though, and slowly Jamie started to move closer again. He leaned forward, wrapping his fingers around her arm, and Anna heard Jen exhale sharply. They'd both been holding their breath.

Then Spark turned, almost flinging herself into Jamie's arms. He hugged her tight for a moment then got her to her feet, moving her away from the tracks. Carefully he helped her back up the embankment, the two figures disappearing behind the trees as they made for the fence.

'Oh! He did it…' Jen shook off Anna's arm and started to jog towards the end of the bridge. Anna let her go. Spark was out of danger now, and the two girls needed each other.

Jamie had wrapped his jacket around Spark's shoulders and was helping her over the low fence, his arm around her as they walked to the pavement. Jen caught up with them, throwing her arms around Spark, and the two girls hugged each other. Anna felt a tear form at the corner of her eye and wiped it away. He was so gentle with the two girls, protecting them both but giving them a little space as well to walk together towards the car.

'Why don't you go and sit in the back of the car for a moment? Then we'll take you back.' Jamie opened the car door and the girls climbed in. Then he turned to Anna.

'She's okay.' He answered the question before she'd had a chance to ask. 'She's cut her arm, but it's not too deep. Maybe you could take a look at it when we get back to the youth centre?'

'Of course. You're not taking her home?'

'She says she doesn't want to go home and I didn't push it with her. I'll give Phil a call now and get him to ring her parents and tell them we've found her. They don't live far from the youth centre and they know us so it might be better if they came there to collect her.'

He took his phone from his pocket and made the call. Then he looked up at Anna, his eyes shining.

'Thank you.'

'It was a privilege to be here. Thanks for trusting me.'

Jamie smiled, a trace of fatigue showing suddenly in his face. 'I honestly never even thought about it. I knew I could rely on you.'

'I'll show you how much I like that you said that.' Anna leaned towards him. 'Later…'

Phil's car drew up outside Jamie's house. Jamie shook his hand, thanking him for all he'd done today, and got out of the car, stretching his legs. As he walked down the drive, he could see that the lights were on in the kitchen. That one, simple thing filled him with warmth. He felt as if he was coming home.

The smell of cooking reached him as he opened the front door. And then Anna walked out of the sitting room to greet him with a kiss. He held her tight, his limbs trembling.

'How did everything go?' Anna looked up at him, her eyes full of concern.

'Good. I think things are going to be fine.' He'd walked out of the youth centre feeling satisfied at a good outcome to the afternoon.

It was what he'd found here that had brought him close to tears.

'You're sure?'

'Yeah. Absolutely.'

'Well, I've made a shepherd's pie and I just need to put it in the oven for half an hour. Then we can eat. Would you like something to drink?'

He followed her into the sitting room. This was turning into a fantasy. Arriving home to find the lights on and a fire in the grate. The smell of cooking and a kiss. Anna wasn't wearing an apron but then aprons were highly overrated. She looked wonderful, her long hair cascading down her back in a blonde shimmering waterfall. All that was missing was the knowledge that there was a sleeping child upstairs who looked just like its mother.

He cleared his throat, trying to shake the picture of a perfect domestic scene. 'I have some beer in the fridge. Would you like some?'

'Yes, I'll join you.' She shot him a smile. 'Sit down, I'll fetch it.'

The temptation was just too much. Jamie lowered himself into a seat in front of the fire and Anna bustled out into the kitchen, returning with two open bottles and two glasses. Instead of just giving him his, she started to pour his beer for him, tilting the glass carefully so that the head didn't fizz up over the top.

'Too much?' The look of mischief in her eyes said it all.

'Yeah. Far too much. I can pour my own beer.'

'I know.' She set the empty bottle down. 'I just thought…'

Jamie chuckled. 'I know what you thought. But you shouldn't wait on me like this. I'm perfectly capable of coming home and making my own dinner, I do it all the time.'

'I can make a bit of a fuss of you, can't I? On a *once in a blue moon* basis?'

'On that basis it's very nice. As long as I get to do the same for you once in a while.'

'Of course.' She smiled brightly handing him the beer, and Jamie put it down onto the table.

'That's yours. I can pour my own.' He caught her hand, pulling her down onto his knee and kissing her. 'That's the only welcome home I really want.'

'What!' She sat up straight in a motion of

mock outrage. 'Are you telling me you don't want my shepherd's pie?'

'I crave your shepherd's pie. It's just that I'd crawl across a hundred of them in order to kiss you.'

'That's all right, then.' She picked up her glass, taking a sip of beer, and leaned back into his arms. 'So tell me what happened after I left this afternoon.'

'Spark's mum asked me to say thank you for the stitches.'

'It was my pleasure. The least I could do for her.'

It wasn't the stitches. It was the care that Anna had shown Spark. No asking her why on earth she'd cut herself or making her feel small. She'd allowed Jen to help her clean the wound, and when she'd finished she'd kissed Spark on the cheek and told her that she was glad she was okay. Anna knew that the hard part was going to be in the conversation that followed, and she'd trusted Jamie and the other staff at the youth centre to do that right.

'Did you see any other scars?'

'A couple, but it didn't look as if the cuts

had been too deep. I don't think she's done it a great deal before now.'

'No, that's what she told me.' He was glad to have Anna's confirmation of that, though.

'And how did things go with her parents? Did they mind that you didn't take her straight home?'

'No, they were fine with that. They know us and I think that they were much more comfortable with having someone there to help mediate. Everyone got to say their piece, and Spark understands how traumatic it was for them when she went missing.'

Anna sighed. 'She must be hurting so much. To do something like that.'

'The worst thing is that she's always been so determined not to show it. When she saw how upset her parents were, I think she realised that they can cope with her grief and she doesn't need to protect them from it. What they can't cope with is her disappearing without a word.'

'Well, I'm glad you're there. For Spark and her parents. Will you be working with them again?'

'Yes, I suggested that they might like to

come to us for family therapy, and her mum and dad were really keen on the idea. I think there are a few things they need to talk about as well.'

'I so wish I could help her.' Anna turned the corners of her mouth down. 'But there are some things that no one can ever put right.'

'Yes and no. We can't bring her brother back, and we can't make all that grief go away. But we don't exist to do that. Our aim is to help show our kids that there's still a way forward.'

Anna fell silent, staring into the fire, her fingers clutching tightly at his shirt. Jamie hugged her, wondering what she was thinking. He was becoming more and more sure that there was something that *she* couldn't put right. Something to do with her marriage, which had hurt her so badly that she'd chosen a way forward that didn't allow for it to ever happen again.

Maybe she'd tell him. He hoped so, because it stood between them, a silent barrier that he couldn't tackle because he didn't know what it was. For the moment, though, he had to be content with just holding her.

'So what about this shepherd's pie, then?'

Anna shook herself out of her reverie. Kissing him, she gave him a bright smile. 'I'll just go and put it in the oven…'

CHAPTER THIRTEEN

'WOULD YOU SHOW me your software?'

'Is that a proposition? Or are you really interested in computers?'

Jamie's soft chuckle sounded from the other end of the phone. 'It would be a proposition if this wasn't a Wednesday. I'm sticking to computers today.'

It was an odd arrangement, but it worked. For the last two and a half weeks Jamie and Anna had been professional whenever they saw each other at the clinic. Never asking about what they were doing that night, never mentioning the Hastings Hustlers, apple pie, or anything else that belonged to the weekend. Never taking the other's presence for granted, because they had their own lives.

The weekends were theirs alone, and they'd become what Anna liked to call *loving friends.* They didn't go on dates. They just did things together. And their nights were full of tenderness and passion.

'Okay. When are you free?' Anna pulled her business diary across the desk.

'Jon's being discharged tomorrow, and I'm going to take him down to Caroline's, he's staying there for a while and travelling back up to London for counselling and to see Dr Lewis. But I'm free after about four o'clock.'

'I have patients until five. Say half five? What exactly do you want to do with my software?'

His quiet laugh wasn't exactly appropriate for a Wednesday. Anna ignored it, because it was so nice. 'We're holding a workshop at the youth centre next week on body image. A few of the kids have asked for one, and it's an issue that affects most of them in one way or another. I was wondering whether you could take me through a typical consultation process and show me the software you use to indicate the difference that surgery will make, so I can answer any questions about that.'

'Fine. No problem, I'll see you then.' Anna adopted a brisk, businesslike tone and Jamie followed suit, confirming the time and giving a brief goodbye.

* * *

He appeared in the doorway of her office at five thirty sharp the following day, holding two coffees. Anna had brushed her hair and refreshed her make-up, but she'd do that for any meeting. Probably. He pushed one coffee across the desk and she thanked him.

'Shall we get started, then? I'll just give you a quick demonstration and you can ask questions as they occur to you.'

Jamie sat down in the chair she'd placed next to hers at her computer. She opened the software, aware suddenly of his scent. Enjoying that was okay as long as she didn't mention it.

'First I need a picture. Hold still a moment and don't smile…' She pointed the camera at the top of the screen at him, and he stared solemnly at it.

'Then I can smooth out any imperfections.' Anna peered at the screen, frowning. She couldn't see anything that she'd want to change about Jamie's face.

'Like the little scar, there?' He pointed to a tiny mark on his forehead.

'Oh, yes. I didn't even see that.' She punched keys, and the scar obligingly disappeared.

'Hmm. I'm not sure that I can tell the difference.' Jamie stared at the screen and Anna smiled.

'I think that's an important point. Everyone has their own idea of what they don't like about themselves, and they assume that everyone else notices those same things. That's not always the case. Plastic surgery can be an objective choice when function is impaired, but in cases where someone simply wants to remove a disfigurement, it's subjective.'

Jamie nodded. 'Yeah. So, in terms of surgery, I've a reasonable idea of what's possible. But what guidelines do you find most useful in advising people?'

'Obviously if it's a matter of restoring the function of a particular part of the body, then it's exactly the same medical considerations you'd use. But cosmetic remodelling is entirely about how the patient feels. Jon's an obvious example.'

'The scars on his face are hardly noticeable now.'

'Yes, exactly. The tissue viability nurse has worked with him to make the skin more comfortable, and he has a very different attitude to them now than when he first came here. Maybe he'll be back to have some work done on them, and maybe not. As long as it's his decision, either choice is okay.'

'I suppose being twins makes a difference.' Jamie leaned back in his seat. 'I've been thinking a bit about how we identify with each other even now.'

Anna nodded. 'Yeah. How you see yourselves as either the same or different is important in a lot of ways.' Jon and Jamie's relationship was changing. They were working things out and there was no longer the push and pull between them that had made their reunion so difficult.

'So, show me a bit more about how the software works.' Jamie leaned forward, studying the screen.

'I'll show you something that I do when I take workshops. I'll take your face as an example.'

'Sure you want to do that?' Jamie grinned at her. He was entirely unaware of his own beauty.

'Well, I'll give it a go. I don't do this with patients, it's just a fun exercise. First of all I can take one half of your face and mirror it.'

Jamie watched as she manipulated the image, raising his eyebrows when Anna frowned.

'What? I can't see any difference.'

'Neither can I. Let me try the other side…' She quickly made a third image, putting it next to the first two on the screen and scanning them. 'Well, it's official, Jamie.'

'What's official? What have you done?' A trace of panic showed in his beautiful eyes.

'You have a perfectly symmetrical face!'

'Is that good?' Jamie had clearly never given his looks much thought.

'It's surprisingly uncommon. Let's try something else. During the Renaissance, painters worked out something called "The Golden Ratio", which mapped out the proportions of a perfect face. Obviously our definition of beauty has changed over time, and there are variations according to different ethnic groups.' This was getting interesting.

'Okay. Do your worst.'

There wasn't a worst to do. Anna was usually able to predict how the results of these simple photo manipulations would turn out, but with Jamie she couldn't. She wondered if maybe subconsciously she'd known…

'Well, that's just outrageous! Did you *know* that you have a perfectly proportioned face?'

He grinned. 'You make it sound like an accusation. And, no, I had no idea.'

'It's really unusual. Mine's way off, I'll show you…'

She reached for the mouse but he pulled it away from her, his expression suddenly serious. 'Your face is perfect. I don't need anything to tell me that you're the most beautiful woman I've ever seen.'

Anna could see in his eyes that he meant it. The temperature in the room seemed to rise suddenly, and playing with pictures of their faces became irrelevant.

'I…guess that's my point. It's impossible to define beauty.' Jamie's was way beyond definition.

'You make your point very well.' Jamie's gaze was still fixed on her face. Anna knew that she wasn't classically beautiful, but he made her feel that way.

'I've got some notes from talks I've done in the past.' The lump in her throat was entirely inappropriate for a work environment. 'Would you like to borrow them?'

'I would, thank you. Or can I persuade you to come and take part in the workshop yourself? It's next Saturday afternoon.'

This was blending their weekends with their jobs. But although she'd tried to keep the two separate, Anna couldn't think of a single reason why she shouldn't.

'I'd really like that. Saturday afternoon, you say?'

He nodded. 'We'll have a few different people giving short presentations, and then we split everyone up into groups to talk.'

'That sounds good. Um… I'll send you my notes, then. They cover some of the more serious issues as well…'

'That's okay. I don't need to see them.' He smiled as Anna's eyebrows shot up. 'I trust you. Just come along and be perfect, the way you always are.'

'I'll drive down on Friday evening?'

Jamie nodded. 'I'd love that.'

The conversation was turning into one of the long, slow seductions that belonged to the weekend. Sitting too close. Staring into each other's eyes as they spoke. A little blurring of the boundaries was acceptable, but this was going a bit too far, and a hint of panic made her hand quiver as she grabbed the mouse. This was her office, and it was supposed to be for work.

'Okay. I'll see you then.' She shut down her computer, aware that his gaze hadn't left her face.

Suddenly he stood. 'Yeah. Thanks for the… demonstration. I appreciate it. I'll look forward to seeing you tomorrow.'

'Yes. Me too.'

He left with a smile, and Anna resisted the temptation to open up her computer again and stare at Jamie's picture. That would be courting trouble, because she could only contemplate their loving friendship if it stayed within the entirely arbitrary rules that they'd set.

'Stupid rules!' She murmured the words to herself, knowing that the rules weren't stupid at all. She could never have all of Jamie, and this arrangement allowed her to have at least part of him. When something good happened, it was wise not to meddle with it.

* * *

Jamie sat at the back of the community room at the youth centre. Community room was a bit of a grand title as it doubled up as a basketball practice court, a chess hall and a large enough area to do any number of things. But at the moment it had just one purpose. Anna was standing at the centre of an arc of chairs, several rows deep, and holding everyone's attention.

She was giving much the same message as the two other speakers, but without the clichés or the solemnity. He'd noticed that Spark and Jen, who were sitting to one side of him, had been fidgeting a bit through the first part of the afternoon, but now they were captivated, turning to each other and nodding from time to time when Anna made an important point.

Jamie was spellbound, too. He knew that Anna had chosen her bright red top to stand out and be seen. That the jokes she made were to reinforce serious points. But he still couldn't take his eyes off her.

She smilingly announced the fun part of her talk, switching on the overhead projector and displaying the picture of herself from her computer, and comparing it with the 'ideal' proportions of a woman's face. She gave herself an electronic rhinoplasty to straighten the slight kink in her nose, which Jamie happened to love very much. She also shaved her jaw, taking out some of the determined air that Jamie also loved. Finally she'd made her eyes bluer, obscuring the pale magic of her gaze.

'What do you all think?' She folded her arms, looking up at her work.

'I prefer the *real* one.' Jen spoke up, waggling her finger at the screen, and Spark nodded. A murmur of agreement went around the hall.

'Well, that's a relief.' Anna grinned. 'And the lesson that I've learned from showing this simple example to a lot of people is that it's the things that are different about us that make us who we are. It's very unusual to find someone who has a perfectly proportioned face, and I'm loving all of the different faces here...'

'And here's a little puzzle for you.' She shot Jamie a momentary glance, and he felt the back of his neck begin to tingle. 'By chance, I happen to know that there is one person here who *does* have a perfectly proportioned face. See if you can guess who it is.'

Everyone looked round and Anna laughed. Jamie saw Spark nudging Jen furiously, and their heads both turned toward him. He chuckled, spreading his hand across his chest in a *who, me?* gesture, and Jen rolled her eyes disbelievingly.

He was going to take some stick for that as soon as Spark and Jen got to share their suspicions with the others. Jamie didn't care. Anna had opened up a conversation, and everyone was thinking about what she'd said and the more serious points she'd made.

There was some lively discussion, and Anna answered the difficult questions that were fired at her honestly and with a large helping of common sense. The speakers were all thanked, and then it was time for drinks before everyone split up into their discussion groups. A group crowded around Anna almost immediately, and he could see her animated and smiling in the centre of it. Jamie knew that a lot of thought had gone into her presentation, and a lot of experience into her answers, but she made it all seem so natural and personal.

He saw Joe's father making his way towards him, while Joe and his mother hung back a bit. 'Hi, Steven. I'm glad you could make it.'

'We wouldn't have missed it, I thought that all the speakers made some very valuable points. Is there any chance that we might have a few words with Miss Caulder?'

'Anna? Yes, of course, I'll go and fetch her. Would you like to go into the sitting room and see her there? It's a bit noisy in here.'

Steven nodded. His son Joe had was eleven years old and the transition from junior to secondary school hadn't been easy for him. He had a dark red birthmark on the side of his neck and jaw, and some of the older kids at his new school had started to bully him. Steven and his wife were at a loss for some direction about what to do about it, and had contacted Jamie about the possibility of counselling.

'You go ahead, then. We'll be with you in a minute.'

Jamie caught Anna's eye, beckoning to her. She smiled, extricating herself from the group of people that surrounded her.

'What did you think?'

She shouldn't even need to ask. 'I thought

you were great. There's someone I'd like you to see, if you don't mind.'

'Of course not, that's what I'm here for. Do I need my laptop?'

'You could bring it along, just in case.'

Anna fetched her laptop, and he led her to the small sitting room that adjoined the hall, quickly telling her about Joe. When they entered, he introduced her to Steven and Josie and she smilingly shook their hands, saving her special smile for Joe.

'Hi, Joe. It's nice to meet you.' She plumped herself down in a chair. 'I hear that you've got some questions for me.'

Steven started to explain, and Anna nodded, watching for Joe's reaction to everything. Haltingly, Joe started to join in, telling her about the bullying. Anna's face darkened.

'And what's the school doing?' She asked the obvious question.

Steven sighed. 'We went to see the headmistress and she said she'd do what she could. She suggested that having the birthmark removed might be a way forward.'

'Oh. Well, I don't think that's a particularly helpful attitude.' Anna's outrage made Steven smile. 'Joe's quite fine as he is, it's the bullies that need to change.'

Slowly but surely she was coaxing Joe out of his shell. He began to talk to her, and then quite of his own accord he got up from his seat, walking over to Anna. 'Do you want to look?' He gestured towards his neck.

'Thank you, Joe. Yes, I'd like to see your birthmark.' Anna waited as Joe took off his sweater and unbuttoned the neck of his shirt. Carefully she examined the skin around his neck and jaw.

'So what do *you* want, Joe?'

The boy frowned. 'Can you show me what I'd look like without it?' He gestured towards Anna's laptop. She glanced at Steven and Josie and Steven nodded.

'Yes, I can do that. Come and sit here beside me and I'll take your picture…'

She was doing it all without suggesting any one solution, letting Joe dictate what he wanted. Jamie saw Josie slip her hand into Steven's as they watched. This was clearly what they'd been waiting for someone to do with Joe.

Anna showed Joe the software first, and then

turned the screen away from him while she altered his photograph. 'Do you have an email address I can send these pictures to, Steven?'

'Yeah.' Steven gestured towards his wife, who quickly pulled pen and paper out of her handbag. 'We really appreciate this, thank you.'

'It's my pleasure.' Anna turned to Joe, tipping the screen towards him so that he could see it. 'I'm going to send these pictures to your dad and so you can have another look at them. If you want to email me back, I'd really like to hear what you think.'

Joe stared at the photographs. Steven and Josie were both holding their breath.

'That's who I am.' Joe pointed at the picture of himself that Anna hadn't altered.

Anna nodded. 'Yes, it is.'

The whole family started to talk. Anna sat back, listening and answering questions. This was what she was really good at—opening avenues of communication.

'Here's my card.' Anna handed Joe one of her cards from the clinic, and he looked at the elegant script. Anna was treating him like a grown-up, and he was responding. The boy who always seemed to be clinging to one or the other of his parents had already gained a little confidence.

'You can get your mum or dad to call me anytime, if there's something you want to talk about.' She glanced at Steven. 'There'll be no cost involved if you want to bring Joe along to see me and discuss his options.'

'I'm sure there should be.' Steven narrowed his eyes. 'But thank you, Miss Caulder.'

'Anna, please. The important thing is that Joe makes his own decision about what he wants to do. When he's done that, I can make a few calls to make sure he gets whatever he needs'

Jamie nodded. 'We can help with that, if necessary.'

'And in the meantime…' Anna moved on smoothly '… I'd like to write a letter to you, outlining some of the things we've talked about today. It's my view that Joe doesn't have an issue with his birthmark, it's the bullying. His headmistress needs to understand that and perhaps a surgeon's letter will reinforce the point.'

'Thank you, Anna. I think that'll really help,

don't you, Steve?' Josie turned to her husband and he nodded in agreement.

'And Joe's having counselling here?' Anna's gaze turned to Jamie.

'Yes, that's right. We'll be seeing you again next week, won't we, Joe?' Jamie reckoned that the counsellor might be speaking to a different boy than the one she'd first met last week. Joe's brief talk with Anna seemed to have set him firmly on the right track, and it was just a matter of following up now.

The chatter from the main hall was subsiding a little, and it was about time for the organisers to divide everyone into discussion groups. Anna reached for her laptop and closed it.

'Is there anything else you'd like to ask? Joe?'

Joe shook his head, and Steven answered. 'We've already kept you long enough. We really appreciate being able to talk to you.'

'It's been my pleasure. I enjoyed meeting you.'

Jamie guided her back to the community room, pointing out the group leaders so that Anna could visit each group and talk to them.

She turned her smile up towards him. 'I'm not enjoying this at all, you know.'

Jamie laughed. 'No, I can see you aren't. They don't love having you here either.'

She gave a mock sigh. 'I suppose it's a boring old evening again afterwards.'

'Yeah. Dry as dust.' Even thinking about it sent shivers of pleasure down Jamie's spine.

'Oh, well. Better get on.' Anna's finger found his hand, her light touch giving him a first taste of the evening ahead. There was an undeniable joy in her step as she walked away from him, making for the first group and sitting down with them.

He didn't need to tell her that she'd done wonders here today—she'd seen it on Joe's face and in the faces of the other kids. She didn't need to tell him that tonight would be anything but dull. It was all unspoken between him and Anna, and that was nice, but Jamie was beginning to want more.

CHAPTER FOURTEEN

EIGHT O'CLOCK ON a Friday evening. Another week had flown by, and the weekend was here again. Jamie heard Anna's car draw up in the drive, and he greeted her at the door. He'd been cooking, and when she stepped into the hallway she wiggled her nose at him.

'I know what you've been up to.'

'Yes. Would you like me to pour you a drink?'

She chuckled, taking off her coat and hanging it on the stand. 'I can pour my own beer, thank you very much.'

'That's not what I had in mind...'

Jamie had never felt as happy as he did now. In the month he and Anna had been together she'd spent every weekend here, with him. They'd come a long way. They'd explored trust, and found that came easily and naturally. Honesty had come naturally too, even if Anna was steadfastly honest about not wanting to talk about her marriage. They'd spent a great deal of time exploring wonderful, tumultuous, tender lovemaking and had shared a hundred everyday things, which felt special when he did them with Anna.

She'd changed him. In ways that he'd never thought possible. And although she was perfect already, there was just one thing that he wanted to change about her.

He led her into the sitting room, gesturing for her to sit down by the fire. He could feel her gaze following him as he walked over to the polished sideboard, from which he'd cleared the usual clutter of books, and switched on the lamp. The light reflected off a row of bottles, a silver ice bucket that he'd found in a junk shop and which had polished up nicely, and two slender glasses.

'Cocktails. I have…um…well, tell me what you want, and I might have it.'

'Mmm.' Anna's gaze ran along the bottles. 'Surprise me.'

That was turning into one of his bounden duties in life. 'Suppose we start with something…as near to virgin as it gets. We can work our way onto something a bit stronger later.'

'Sounds good to me.'

Jamie measured out the liquids, pouring them carefully so that the rainbow effect of the different densities of liquid wasn't disturbed. A dash of spirits, and then a cherry on top. He carried the drinks over to the sofa, and they sat down together.

'This is all very nice.' She took a sip from her glass. 'And that's lovely. So what's the occasion?'

Jamie grinned. 'Oh, it's Friday evening. You've been working hard all week, and you've just driven all the way down from London.'

'That's it?'

'Well, I know it's not my birthday. It's not yours, is it?' He knew so little of the minutiae of Anna's life, but still he felt he knew everything about her.

'No.' She slipped off her shoes, tucking her legs up underneath her. 'Although if it meant getting one of your foot massages, I could always change it.'

'It's Friday. That's sufficient excuse for a foot massage.'

'Ah, wonderful.' She leaned forward, kissing him. 'You are a dream.'

Jamie wanted to be *more* than just a dream. He wanted to be part of Anna's reality. But he'd ask about that later.

'We'll eat first, though? I'm not planning on stopping with just your feet…'

'Mmm. Good idea. Do you want a hand?'

'No, everything's sorted. Just relax in here for ten minutes and then we'll eat.'

It was really nice of him. He'd made a tasty chicken casserole with roast potatoes, and they ate in the dining room rather than the kitchen. There was a snowy white tablecloth, heavy silver cutlery and candles on the table, and after crème brûlée for dessert he served coffee.

'There's something I wanted to ask you.' His eyes were sparkling in the flickering candlelight and he looked so handsome. Anna was sure that her answer was going to be *yes*.

'What is it?'

'We've been seeing each other for a month now. We've shared so much and… I want you to trust me.'

A flutter of uneasiness beat suddenly in

her chest, and it occurred to Anna that this wasn't going to be the automatic *yes* that she'd thought. 'Trust you? With what?'

'I want you to trust me enough to tell me what hurt you so badly. You always say that your marriage is in the past, but I know there's something you can't break free from.'

The flutter became a determined beat of panic. Jamie had asked before, but there was something about his manner that told Anna he wasn't going to back off this time.

'I don't want to talk about it, Jamie.'

She *couldn't* talk about it. If she told him why Daniel had left her then he'd know that she couldn't have children. Maybe he'd say that he didn't care, and she'd believe him. Anna suddenly realised that it would hurt a great deal more if Jamie did as Daniel had done, accepted her as she was and then changed his mind. And he *would* change his mind, Jamie so obviously wanted kids of his own.

He was shaking his head slowly. 'I need to know, Anna. What we have now…'

She stared at him. What they had now was suddenly changing. She dreaded it, but it seemed unstoppable.

'I need to know that you trust me, the way I trust you.' His voice was as gentle as a lover's sigh. 'I made one huge mistake when I blundered blindly into a relationship with Gill, and… I want ours to be different.'

'But…' Anna shivered. He'd used the 'R' word, and they'd promised not to do that. It seemed Jamie had already found a promise to go back on. 'We said this *wasn't* a relationship, didn't we?'

'Yeah, I know. But things change, Anna. I think about you all the time, and I want to share everything with you. You've changed me on a level that I just didn't realise anyone had access to. And I love being with you.'

He reached forward, catching her hand and pressing her fingers to his lips. Despite herself, Anna smiled.

'I love being with you, too.'

He took one ragged breath, his gaze tender. 'All I've been thinking about lately is a future with you, Anna. I know that's not what we agreed, and if you're not ready for that it's okay. But if you are… I want you to know that I'm ready for it too.'

Anna squeezed her eyes shut and shook her

head. She'd hung onto the notion that she and Jamie would never get to the point of having this conversation. That he was as damaged as she was, and that they could continue on together with no thought of commitment or the future. But it seemed that somewhere along the way Jamie had done some healing.

'Okay. That's fair enough. Whenever you're ready.'

She was never going to be ready. Jamie might have moved forward, but Anna couldn't.

'Look, Jamie, I know that you've been through a lot, and I'm really glad that you feel that you can put that behind you now. And I know you believe that it's possible to mend things in the future…' Anna shook her head.

He gave her an uncomprehending look. 'I *have* to believe it. I believed it when I went to medical school, and managed to stay the course despite my dyslexia. And the kids I work with are making better futures for themselves, too.'

'There are some things you can't mend, Jamie. They're just facts of life and it's not possible to make them any different. You just have to accept them.'

'So…you won't even accept that we might have a chance? I don't understand, Anna.'

Jamie wasn't going to give up. She was going to have to tell him. She was going to have to see the look on his face before she could fully believe that he was capable of breaking her heart.

'Jamie, the reason my marriage broke up was because I can't have children. My husband knew that right from the start, and he said that he was fine with it. A year after we got married he suddenly decided he wasn't fine with it after all and he left me.'

He stared at her. Somewhere deep down she'd still believed in a fairy-tale world where it wouldn't matter and she could love Jamie the way she wanted to. But then she saw it. Denial.

'Are you sure?'

A tear rolled down her face. This was the beginning of an end that couldn't be averted now.

'Yes, I'm sure. I'm a surgeon, Jamie, do you really think that I haven't explored all the options?'

He was staring at her, shaking his head. Jamie never gave up, and she loved him for it.

The trouble was that he didn't know when he was beaten either.

'I have a congenital abnormality that affects both my Fallopian tubes and my uterus. I can't have children.'

'I don't care.'

He was still holding on. Still believing in a future that just couldn't happen.

'Have you ever thought you might have children?'

He shrugged. 'Well, yes, of course, but—'

'But nothing! I've seen you with your niece and nephews, you love them. You're going to make a great dad, but you can't do it with me.' Anna stood up. She had to go. There wasn't enough air in the room and she was going to suffocate if she stayed.

'Wait. Anna, will you stop second-guessing me? Can you give me a moment to process this, and then we can talk about it?'

Talking wasn't going to change anything. 'No, because you're going to tell me that it doesn't matter—'

'Right in one. It doesn't.' His face darkened with anger.

'And then I'll believe you. And I'll believe

we have a future. Don't you dare make me do that, Jamie, because I know for sure that it's going to break me when you come to your senses and decide you want a family of your own.'

'Sit down!'

'Do *not* tell me what to do, Jamie. We never promised each other anything, and I'm leaving now. I won't be back.'

Anger propelled Anna out into the hallway. She picked up her coat and the overnight bag that she'd left there when she'd come in tonight, and ran out to her car. She couldn't stay. She couldn't face his disappointment or his pity or whatever else it was he had to throw at her. She just had to get away.

Jamie stared blankly at the table in front of him. She wouldn't. Anna couldn't.

The silence that had seemed to damn him in Anna's eyes had been shock. Sudden understanding of all the little things he'd wondered about. But she'd seen it as rejection. She'd think about that for a moment and realise she was wrong and turn around so that he could tell her the one obvious truth. He could give up anything else in his life as long as Anna stayed…

Then he heard the front door bang. When he walked to the window, he saw the headlights of her car flip on and then slowly arc across the driveway.

He could have borne whatever Anna cared to throw at him. He could have borne her silence. But he couldn't bear it that she'd just left before he'd even had a chance to take in everything she'd said properly.

Gill had done that too. He knew now that there had been a lot wrong with their relationship, and it was unlikely that anything either of them could have said would have mended it. But she'd never allowed him the opportunity of any understanding or closure. Had just walked away. And now Anna, the person he believed in more than anyone else he'd ever known, had done the same thing. They could have made it work, but she wouldn't even try.

Perhaps she'd feel differently about it in the morning. It was a great thought, but Jamie knew that it was never going to happen. He could call and she wouldn't answer. He might even sit down and laboriously write an email, setting out everything he wanted to say to her, but he'd never know if she'd even read it because she wouldn't reply. Once Anna had made up her mind about something she stuck to it.

Anger coursed through his veins. So much for candlelight and a nice dinner. He pinched the wicks of the candles to extinguish them, cursing when he burned his fingers. Then in a sudden blind rage, directed at himself, Anna, and the rest of the world, he swept his arm across the table. Plates and candlesticks went flying, hitting the floor with a crash, which somehow didn't satisfy him as much as it should have. Walking out of the house, he stood on the veranda, shivering and watching the rain fall.

When Anna popped her head around the door of the waiting room, Callum and his aunt were sitting alone. She'd expected that—she hadn't seen or heard from Jamie in the last three weeks. That was partly due to the fact that she'd been judiciously avoiding him.

This would be the last time she'd go through this kind of heartbreak. She'd been with Jamie for four short weeks, but in that time she'd known he was the love of her life. 'The One.' If it was impossible for her to stay with him, then there would never be anyone else. She'd never be hurt again.

Callum looked up and saw her, giving her a smile. Anna switched on the smile she'd been hiding behind ever since she'd walked out on Jamie.

'Hi, Callum. How are you doing?'

'Great. Thanks.'

He didn't look great. That was generally the case with patients who came for a second laser treatment for tattoo removal, they knew what to expect this time. She beckoned for him to follow her and his aunt gathered up her coat and came too.

'So. Let's take a look at your hand, then.'

Callum brightened a bit. 'It's looking really good, don't you think?'

Anna examined his hand carefully. All of the inflammation had gone down now, and the tattoos were now a faded collection of disjointed lines with no discernible meaning.

'Yes, I'm really pleased with the results, these should only need one more treatment and then we can get started on the other hand. Generally tattoos need a great deal more work before they fade, but these small amateur tattoos are sometimes easier to remove than professional ones, because of the depth of penetration and type of ink.'

Callum grinned. 'I'll remember that for the future.'

Anna glanced at Callum's aunt, who had frowned suddenly in response to her nephew's joke. She felt a tingle at the back of her neck. A remembered reaction to the expected interjection from Jamie. But he wasn't here.

'You have to think very carefully before getting any tattoo, Callum. I'd say that if removal even crosses your mind, that's a pretty solid reason not to get one done in the first place.'

Callum nodded. 'I've learned my lesson. I won't be getting any more. Jamie said I should focus on how my hands are going to look when this is finished, and how I'm going to keep them that way.'

Anna resisted the temptation to ask Callum exactly where and when he'd last seen Jamie, and how he was. 'Yes, that's a good suggestion.'

'He said to say hello.'

'Did he?' Anna obviously hadn't managed to conceal her surprise and consternation because Callum shrugged.

'Well, he didn't actually *say* it. I expect he forgot. I'll tell him hello back, shall I?'

Anna thought quickly. Maybe the Hastings Hustlers had noticed something and this was a heavy-handed attempt to open the lines of communication between her and Jamie again. On the other hand, Callum might just be trying to be polite, it was difficult to tell.

'How is he?'

'Okay. Pretty much the same as always.'

'Right. Well, I'm glad to hear it. Don't bother to tell him hello, I should probably give him a call. I'll say hello myself.'

'Okay.' Callum turned his attention back to his hand. He clearly had more important things on his mind and he was looking nervous again.

Jamie was right, fixing his attention on the results of the procedure would help Callum through the discomfort. Even now, after everything they'd been through, Jamie was still there in her head. The worst part of it was that even though it hurt, she welcomed it because it was the last thing she had left of him.

'Right. Would you like to say goodbye to these?' She smiled at Callum, indicating the remnants of the tattoos. 'It may well be the last you'll see of them.'

Callum laughed. 'Good riddance more like.'

'I think so too. Let's get started…'

'What do you think?' Jon handed Jamie the playlist, which had been typed in double spacing to make it easier to read. Jamie studied it carefully.

'That'll be great. You're accompanying "Everywhere" on the mandolin?'

'Yes, that was a great suggestion of yours. Just right for the unplugged version.'

Jamie and Jon were sitting in armchairs on either side of the fireplace, where a blazing fire was chasing away the chill of an October evening. Good food, long tramps in the countryside and intensive counselling had done their work, and Jon was looking a great deal better now.

'You're sure this isn't too soon? You don't *have* to get straight back to work, you know.'

Jon shrugged. 'I know. I really want to do it, though. Getting back to my roots a bit, playing small venues with a few new arrangements of the songs. It's only going to be four dates, and I'm really looking forward to it.'

'Well, I'll be keeping an eye on you.'

'That's another thing I'm looking forward to. Having my big brother keep an eye on me.'

They'd come a long way together. They'd talked about everything, all of the things that had gradually built up resentment and pushed them apart. Then finally they'd talked about Gill. Jamie had acknowledged that his relationship with his ex-fiancée had been quietly deteriorating for some time, and Jon had acknowledged that his behaviour had been inexcusable. Then they'd forgiven each other.

'Caroline says she's coming along, to the final gig. She's bringing Jessica.'

Jamie chuckled. 'Doesn't that make you feel old? That your niece is grown up enough to come to one of your concerts?'

'I quite like it. Feels like a new lease of life.' Jon stretched his arms out, holding his hands towards the fire.

'I hope it's not going to be too cold.'

'Nah. Big tent in the park. What's not to

like? If anyone gets frostbite I'll hand them over to you.'

'Because it's always useful to have a doctor around?' Jamie smiled.

'Yep. You can never have too many doctors.' Jon frowned suddenly. 'I wanna say something.'

That usually meant it was something that he didn't want to hear. But Jamie felt numb these days. The pain of missing Anna had made everything else seem trivial. 'Yeah, go ahead.'

'It's none of my business…'

'Whatever. Say it anyway.'

'You're bloody miserable, mate. Caroline's noticed as well.'

Jamie stared at his brother. Since he hadn't spoken about his affair with Anna, he'd told himself that no one need know about the break-up. Silence had been his way of keeping it all together, because it hurt too much to put into words. Clearly he hadn't made as good a job of covering his feelings as he'd thought.

'I'm okay.'

'Yeah, pull the other one. One minute you and Anna are joined at the hip, and you're looking like the cat that's got the cream. The next minute she's gone and… Look, I'm the last person who should be mentioning your love life to you.'

Jamie shrugged. 'Didn't we say that we were going to put that in the past? Now that we both understand a little more about why it happened, we can let it go.'

'That's what *you* said. And I'll always be grateful for it, because it's given us a future. That's not my point, Jamie. My point is that when I hit rock bottom it was because I'd lost my faith in anything ever changing. You were the one who showed me I was wrong.'

'It's complicated, Jon.'

'It always is. Until it's not.'

Jamie didn't answer. He didn't want to think about it, because Anna had been the best thing that had ever happened to him. And losing her had been the worst.

He stared into the fire, watching the flames dance. Anna had taken his heart when she'd walked away. He'd been angry, and she probably didn't even know that he'd do anything to be with her.

An idea occurred to him. It was crazy, a chance in a million… But it had been a long time since the Campbell-Clarke brothers had taken their one chance in a million, made a song out of it, and it had shaped both their futures.

'There is something…'

Jon looked up at him. 'Yeah? Name it, big brother.'

CHAPTER FIFTEEN

EVERYONE AT THE clinic was talking about Jonny Campbell's new song. It had been released free on the internet, and in the first few hours had been downloaded over a million times. When Anna had listened to it, it had made her cry. 'Whatever' was a love song. One that promised a true and faithful heart. Whatever the cost and whatever happened.

The ticket had arrived by courier, and Anna had been called down to the clinic's reception desk to sign for it personally. There was a note inside from Jon, asking her to come to the first of four concerts, which would be taking place in one of the central London parks, the following week.

She couldn't go, of course. She'd made discreet enquiries, and it seemed that no one else at the clinic had received a ticket so she'd been singled out. If Jamie was behind it, it would only lead to more heartbreak.

But she couldn't shake the words of the song. It had the same haunting quality as 'Everywhere'. What if Jamie had written it?

The Saturday of the concert was a bright, clear day, and Anna couldn't help herself. She had to go. Whatever the cost, and whatever happened.

There had been a frenzied demand for tickets, and security was tight at the entrance to the area where the tent was pitched. She'd heard that it held a thousand people, and it was enormous, with a stage at one end ringed by security. Her ticket got her into the front section, just yards from the stage.

Excitement hung in the air, and Anna stood alone to one side, watching the hubbub around her. The promise of new, 'unplugged' versions of Jonny Campbell's greatest hits had attracted both young and old, and there was a friendly, almost holiday atmosphere. Anna felt sick from the cacophony of feelings that were tugging her in so many different directions. She was about to leave when a roar went up and the crowd surged forward as Jon stepped out onto the stage.

He looked good. There was a spring in his

step and he'd lost the haggard, disconnected look that he'd had when he'd first checked into the clinic. He'd ditched his signature leather trousers in favour of jeans and a casual shirt, but he hadn't been able to resist a leather jacket, lined with studs across the back. The scars on his face were still there, but they seemed less vivid against the healthy colour of his face. It was good to see the change in him.

He started to speak, thanking everyone for coming, and receiving a cheer in response. There were a few jokes and some banter with the crowd, and then Anna froze.

'My brother Jamie is half an hour older than me, and a great deal better looking. He wrote "Everywhere" when we were eighteen, and since then we've been through a lot together. So it's my great pleasure to welcome him here this afternoon...'

She wanted to run, but that would only draw attention to herself. And this was what she was here for, wasn't it? She'd been drawn like a moth to the flame, needing to find out if this new song was what she didn't dare hope it might be. She pulled the woollen hat she'd brought with her from her pocket, putting it on and stepping behind a group of people so she couldn't be spotted from the stage.

There was a cheer when Jamie came onto the stage, and he acknowledged it diffidently, sitting down on one of the two high stools at the front of the stage and picking up a guitar. Jon joined him, reaching for a mandolin, and the two of them started to play.

The new arrangement of 'Everywhere' was more beautiful than the original. Anna couldn't tear her gaze from Jamie. He was so close, but she knew he couldn't see her, and she felt tears of frustration and uncertainty run down her face.

'You like this version?'

A roar of approval answered Jon's question and he laughed, caught up by the sheer delight of being on stage.

'Okay, it'll be released in a couple of weeks. Jamie wrote "Everywhere" sixteen years ago, and it's taken a very special lady to make him pick up his pen again. Anna, if you're here, this one's for you…'

Everyone was looking around. Anna felt her cheeks burn. 'Whatever' really was her song? Jamie seemed determined not to look at the crowd, and walked over to the piano, sitting down to play the first few chords. Jon began to sing, and was walking up and down at the front of the stage, seeming to be scanning the audience.

Suddenly she knew. The song said everything. Jamie wanted her, and he'd always love her. He could give up anything else in his life, but he couldn't lose her. Anna waved, desperately trying to catch his attention, to show him that she was here, but he seemed oblivious of everything but the piano keys. But Jon saw her, and signalled to one of the security men around the stage. The man cleared a path through for her, and she ran forward.

'Jamie! *Jamie!*' He had to look up and see her.

Jon stopped singing, leaving the backing players to continue with the melody. Then Jamie looked up and saw her. His reaction was immediate, and he ran to the edge of the stage.

'Looks as if my brother's got something more important on his mind than playing the piano. I'm gonna need some help. Do we have the words…?' Jon looked round at the screen that was suspended over his head and the precious words, which were all for her, flashed up. He started to sing again, and the crowd joined in. Jamie jumped down from the stage, and Anna flung herself into his arms.

'You didn't look for me?' She had to press her lips close to his ear so that he could hear her.

'I was too afraid you wouldn't be there. I had to ask Jon to do it for me.' He kissed her and suddenly everything was all right.

'Do you really mean it, Jamie? That you'll love me whatever happens?'

'Of course I mean it. I've just said it in front of a thousand people, and I was going to keep saying it until you heard me. Loving you isn't just what I do, it's who I am.'

'It's who I am, too. I love you, Jamie.'

Somewhere, far away, the crowd was cheering. But Jamie was kissing her, and nothing else mattered.

EPILOGUE

Three years later

'JON'S ASKED ME if I'm going to write another song.'

'And are you?'

'Nah. The only songs I'll be writing any time soon are lullabies.'

Anna and Jamie were curled up together on their bed. It was early still, but they couldn't take their eyes off the two cradles by the side of the bed, where their one-week-old twins were sleeping.

'We're so lucky, Jamie. Everything worked out.'

'You thought it wouldn't?'

'I knew it would. But I'm so happy it worked out like this.'

When they'd got married, Jamie and Anna had promised to love each other and trust in the future. And the future had repaid their trust and given them more than they ever could have hoped for. Tests had shown that although she couldn't conceive or carry a baby, Anna could produce viable eggs. Caroline had been the one to suggest that she could act as a surrogate for them and their twins, a girl and a boy, had been safely delivered last week.

'I don't think I'll ever be able to thank Caroline enough.' Anna snuggled against Jamie's chest.

'I think you've mentioned that to her. Once or twice. And even if you hadn't I think that your offer to look after her kids for two weeks, while she and Harry have a holiday together next summer, was nothing short of heroic.'

'You don't mind, do you?'

'Mind? I'll be camping out in the garden with the boys. You and Jess can make your own arrangements.'

'I thought I might take her for a pamper day. Get our hair and nails done maybe.'

Jamie chuckled. 'She'll like that. You think we could persuade Caroline and Harry to make it three weeks?'

'We could try. You never know.'

Never knowing had become one of Anna's

greatest joys. They hadn't known that the up dated version of 'Everywhere' would outsell the original, and help finance the expansion of Jamie's charity, allowing him to devote all his time to it. Or that the London Central Clinic would offer her a two-days-a-week contract so that she could spend more time at home, enjoying being a mum. Or that Jon would finally find some peace, and was managing to combine a successful solo career with a stable home life.

'Jen called me yesterday. She's got the day off work and she and Spark are coming over. She said she hoped I hadn't bought any more sleepsuits.'

Jamie winced. 'Tell me they haven't decided on skulls and crossbones this time…'

'I wouldn't like to make any promises. Since she's been on that textiles course at college, Spark can make just about anything.'

'Yeah. The Hastings Hustlers sleepsuits she made are great. I can't wait to show them off to the team.' Jamie folded her in his arms, hugging her tight. 'I can't wait for any of it, Anna. As long as it's with you.'

Anna laughed, kissing him. 'That's just as

well, because you're stuck with me now. I'm not going anywhere.'

'That's all I'll ever want, Anna. You're stuck with me, too. Always.'

Whatever happened. They'd completed the process of being vetted as adoptive parents, so there might well be more children to share their love with. The charity was growing, and Jamie had set innovative programmes into motion that had caught the attention of other youth agencies. The future was an endless stream of possibilities and Jamie's restless energy was tempered by an obvious contentment, which matched Anna's own.

'What's that tune?' Jamie was humming something that didn't sound familiar.

'I'm not sure.' He hummed another few bars of the melody, and then sang a few words. '"*You never know...*"'

'I thought you weren't going to write another song.' She grinned at him.

'I couldn't help it. It just popped into my head.' He kissed her forehead and then started humming again.

Anna reached for her phone, switching on

the audio recorder. 'Here, sing it again before you forget it.'

He hummed the tune again, with a few more words this time, and then switched the recorder off, putting the phone down on the bed. 'I do know one thing.'

'Me too.'

They both knew that they loved each other, and their beautiful babies. And that was the only thing that either of them needed.

* * * * *

LET'S TALK
Romance

For exclusive extracts, competitions and special offers, find us online:

- facebook.com/millsandboon
- @millsandboonuk
- @millsandboon

Or get in touch on 0844 844 1351*

For all the latest titles coming soon, visit millsandboon.co.uk/nextmonth

*Calls cost 7p per minute plus your phone company's price per minute access charge